RHAPSODY
IN STEPHEN'S GREEN

RHAPSODY
IN STEPHEN'S GREEN

THE INSECT PLAY

Flann O'Brien
(Myles na gCopaleen)

Edited, with introduction and notes
by Robert Tracy

THE LILLIPUT PRESS
MMXI

Copyright © Evelyn O'Nolan, Robert Tracy, W.J. Mc Cormack 1994

First published in 1994 by
THE LILLIPUT PRESS LTD
62—63 Sitric Road, Arbour Hill,
Dublin 7, Ireland

Reprinted with amendments, 2011

A CIP record for this
title is available from
The British Library

ISBN 978 1 874675 27 3
Series editor: W.J. Mc Cormack

Cover design by Ed Miliano

Set in 10 on 12 Palatino by Koinonia of Manchester
and printed in Dublin by eprint limited, Blanchardstown

CONTENTS

SERIES EDITOR'S PREFACE

This series called ETCH, Essays and Texts in Cultural History, fills the gap between short articles in obscure journals and lengthy books at inflated prices. The field is the cultural history of Ireland in the broadest sense, including work both in Gaelic and English, non-literary material and foreign commentary. It includes essays, commissioned reprints of valuable items from the past, translations . . . any kind of material which can increase our awareness of cultural history as it affects Ireland.

When the ETCH series published a selection of brief texts by Daniil Kharms, comparison was made between the absurd world of the Russian absurdist and that of the Irish novelist, Flann O'Brien. Not everyone was pleased by the implied similarity, as if the comparative method robbed the local boy of some of his distinction. The present number in the series answers any provincialism of that kind by making available O'Brien's idiosyncratic version of a famous play by the Czech dramatist, Karel Čapek. The two authors shared the experience of witnessing the coming into being of an independent state (the Czech republic, the Irish Free State) in the aftermath of the Great War. If further mediation between them were required one has only to consider the novels of Franz Kafka, in which a logic as inescapable and elusive as that of *The Third Policeman* had earlier been confronted in *The Trial* and *The Castle*. The world of central European urban alienation may seem remote from O'Brien's parodic, raucous provincials, and yet Kafka had been introduced to the English-speaking world by a translator (Edwin Muir) born in the Orkney Islands. Relations between the various epicentres of literary modernism cannot be measured in miles or kilometres, and *Rhapsody in Stephen's Green* proceeds in the irreverent confidence that the setting had been claimed by Joyce's alter ego as 'my green' even before the Great War began. In Robert Tracy the dramatic side of O'Brien has found a suitably polyglot advocate, one who is at home in the Slavic languages and who is no respecter of parish boundaries.

INTRODUCTION

Aristotle's remarks on comedy. Books XI-XX and XLVI-CXLII of Livy's *History*. The later books of *The Faerie Queene*. Byron's memoirs. The first version of Carlyle's *French Revolution*. Parts 2 and 3 of *Dead Souls*. The last six numbers of *The Mystery of Edwin Drood*. These are among the most celebrated items in the tantalizing Alexandrian library of unread texts, that mysterious depository of lost works. Until now, *Rhapsody in Stephen's Green (The Insect Play)* by Myles na gCopaleen has been listed among them. Myles's critics and biographers have mentioned the play, describing it as an adaptation from an earlier work by Karel and Josef Čapek. They have speculated about its content, drawing on reviews and recollections of the 1943 Dublin production, and on the fortunate survival of Act I among the Myles Papers now owned by the University of Southern Illinois.[1]

As it happens, the rest of the play has also survived, thanks to Hilton Edwards and Micheál MacLiammóir, who carefully preserved scripts and drawings during their fifty years (1928-78) together operating Dublin's Gate Theatre, and to librarians at Northwestern University, Illinois, who purchased the Gate Theatre archive. My own interest in the Edwards-MacLiammóir years at the Gate, and especially their productions of Chekhov, led me to the Northwestern collection's catalogue, where, with the excitement of James's 'publishing scoundrel' hovering over the desk that might contain Jeffrey Aspern's letters, or of Colonel Isham about to open the croquet box at Malahide Castle, I spotted *The Insect Play*. Would it be only the already published Act I? An obliging brother-in-law went to see. The Gate archive contains a typescript of the complete play, marked with stage directions and deletions by Hilton Edwards, and evidently used as the prompt copy.

'One beginning and one ending for a book was a thing I did not agree with,' declares the narrator of Flann O'Brien's *At Swim-Two-Birds* (1939); 'A good book may have three openings entirely

dissimilar and interrelated only in the prescience of the author. . .
O'Brien proceeds to demonstrate the principle, and to make great
play with triads throughout that extraordinary novel. But he
also employed the principle in life, at least in his literary life.
Flann O'Brien was born on 13 March 1939, on the title page of *At
Swim-Two-Birds*, and went on to write three more novels: *The Hard
Life* (1961); *The Dalkey Archive* (1964); and *The Third Policeman*,
apparently written around 1940, but not published until 1967.

But Flann O'Brien was also Myles na gCopaleen and Brian
O'Nolan, occasionally assuming yet other identities. Myles na
gCopaleen, Myles of the Little Horses, or, as he himself was to
insist, Myles of the Ponies, was born in 1829, as the resourceful
and loquacious horse-trader in Gerald Griffin's melodramatic
novel *The Collegians*. He was born again three times: as the leading
character in Dion Boucicault's play *The Colleen Bawn* (1860), freely
adapted from Griffin's novel; as a tenor role in Sir Julius
Benedict's opera *The Lily of Killarney* (1862), adapted from Griffin
and Boucicault; and finally, yet again, in October 1940, when
Brian O'Nolan borrowed his identity to write a column for *The
Irish Times*. It is appropriate that this 'lost' play should have been
written by a man who did not exist.

As for Brian O'Nolan, who spent many years in Ireland's Civil
Service,[2] the Registrar of Births, Deaths, and Marriages records his
birth — as Brian Nolan — at Strabane, County Tyrone, on 1
October 1911, his marriage in Dublin in 1948, and his death in 1966
— on April Fools' Day. The shamrock, after all, triple-leaved,
three-in-one, is Ireland's emblem.

From the commencement of his *Irish Times* column, Myles
became a familiar presence in Dublin. Originally written in Irish,
usually in English after 1944, but sometimes in Latin or French,
the column grew in popularity and notoriety, as did its recurring
characters and motifs: the aristocratic Sir Myles na gCopaleen (the
da); Keats and Chapman; the Brother ('The Brother says the seals
near Dublin do often come up out of the water at nighttime and do
be sittin above in the trams . . .'); the Myles na gCopaleen Central
Research Bureau; the Cruiskeen Court of Voluntary Jurisdiction;
the District Court; Myles's concerns about the maintenance and
treatment of locomotives belonging to the Great Northern
Railway.

But the central concern was always language, its use and misuse, even when Myles was only amusing himself by parading technical terms from *The Steam Boiler Year Book and Manual*. His commitment to the integrity of language, and disdain for its misuse — especially by politicians — invites comparison with another great journalist, the Viennese Karl Kraus (1874-1936). Myles's column began as a sardonic commentary on the official Irish that had become compulsory in schools and in the Civil Service after the establishment of the Irish Free State in 1922. The son of an Irish-speaking household at a time when, in one of his own favorite phrases, the Irish language 'was neither profitable nor popular', he scorned the stiff Civil Service Irish that came into use, and was quick to spot the frequent mistakes made by new users of the language. Promoters of 'Revival Irish' tended to spend time in rural areas that were still, more or less, Irish-speaking, but were also places of great poverty. Being a peasant, being miserably poor, and speaking Irish became equivalents, supposedly defining those who were truly representative of the Irish nation and its values — those who had what Abbey Theatre actors came to call *P.Q.*, peasant quality. The only novel he published as Myles na gCopaleen, *An Béal Bocht* (1941), written in Irish, parodies revered peasant autobiographies: Tomás O Criomhthain's *An tOileánach* (1929; *The Islandman*); Peig Sayers's *Peig* (1939); and Muiris O Súilleabháin's *Fiche Blian ag Fás* (1933; *Twenty Years a-Growing*). These autobiographies describe the poverty-stricken and sometimes dangerous lives of their authors on the remote western seaboard. In Ireland *an béal bocht*, the poor mouth, describes someone who is always talking about his own miserable circumstances, but Myles also used the phrase to remind his readers that the poorest of their fellow citizens, living in great squalor, were those native speakers of Irish so admired by well-fed and well-housed middle-class enthusiasts for the revival of the Irish language — *lá breá*, fine day, as they were derisively called, from their habit of shouting out that phrase to laboring men and women as they sauntered about the *Gaeltacht* (Irish-speaking area) in summer. Myles loved the Irish language, but had little respect for Gaelic League enthusiasts.

Irish nationalists and Irish writers have been preoccupied with basic questions about language, at least since Douglas Hyde's

1892 manifesto, 'The Necessity for De-Anglicizing Ireland.' A year later Hyde founded the Gaelic League, dedicated to maintaining Irish as a spoken language. Subsequently, while some language activists envisaged the ultimate replacement of English by Irish, official statements avoided, or saw no reason for, a clear definition of the overall linguistic goal. For most Irish writers the demand that they abandon the language they habitually speak and write, English, has been a provocative challenge rather than an imperative. French writers do not have to consider whether or not they should write in French, nor do German writers need to ponder their right to use German. Some Irish writers did and do write in Irish, like the great novelist Máirtín Ó Cadhain (1906-1970), or the poet Nuala Ní Dhomhnaill. Most writers follow Yeats by continuing to write in English, sometimes, as with Synge and Lady Gregory, adapting English words to Irish grammatical structures. Joyce records Stephen Dedalus's uneasiness as he talks with the English-born Dean of Studies in *Portrait*; Joyce solved the English/Irish problem for himself by inventing his own polyglot language in *Finnegans Wake*. Beckett chose to write in French, and revered silence. Most Irish writers, then, have responded to the controversy about what language they should use by becoming self-conscious about language, and often making language itself their theme, almost their protagonist. Myles does so in Acts I and III of *Rhapsody in Stephen's Green*.

Though Myles began at *The Irish Times* by parodying and ridiculing those who misused Irish, he was soon considering misuses and abuses of English as well. A dictionary of clichés became a regular feature of his column:

Is man ever hurt in a motor smash?
No. He sustains an injury.
Does such a man ever die from his injuries?
No. He succumbs to them.

Of what was any deceased citizen you like to mention typical?
Of all that is best in Irish life.
Correct. With what qualities did he endear himself to all who knew him?
His charm of manner and unfailing kindness.

4

Till what great dairy-farm re-union may you sit and talk there?
Till the cows come home.

De quibus non curat lex?
Minimis.
Quideat emptor?
Cave.[3]

In one memorable column Myles compared the English and Irish texts of the Irish Constitution, claiming that 'Some of the English is bad and most of the Irish is disgracefully bad. More, the two languages frequently express dissimilar and mutually repugnant meanings in stating what purports to be the same Article. If we fail to make the most of such little English as we now remember,' he wrote on another occasion, 'it may bode ill for us . . . There *are* still tribes old-fashioned enough to take the view that intelligible talk is one way by which one can distinguish humanity . . .'[4] Like Joyce, whose 'Epiphanies' recorded exchanges or remarks overheard in the streets of Dublin, Myles liked to present the banalities of 'the plain people of Ireland'. His Keats and Chapman pieces were carefully constructed to culminate in an atrocious pun on some often-repeated phrase. A short story, 'The Martyr's Crown', is about a woman who became pregnant because she went to bed with a British officer in 1916, thus preventing him from searching her house and finding the rebels hiding upstairs. The story ends with a glimpse of the son of that union, and the inevitable but unexpected inversion: 'thousands . . . of Irish men and women have died for Ireland . . . But that young man was *born* for Ireland.'[5]

Flann O'Brien was the author of novels only. Myles na gCopaleen wrote *The Irish Times* column, but was also the author of three plays. *Thirst*, in one act, was written for inclusion in *Jack-in-the-Box*, the Gate Theatre's 1942 Christmas entertainment. *Faustus Kelly*, in three acts, opened at the Abbey on 25 January 1943 and ran for two weeks. *Rhapsody in Stephen's Green*, commissioned by Hilton Edwards, was performed by the Gate Company at Dublin's Gaiety Theatre from 22 March to 27 March 1943. Later Myles wrote four plays, and a fifteen-episode television series, for RTE, the Irish television company.

Flann O'Brien's novels have all been successfully adapted for the stage by other hands. Myles had one of the dramatist's essential gifts, the ability to write dialogue, especially dialogue that is at once banal and entertaining. He had a remarkable ear for local dialects of Irish-English: Trinity College English, Dublin English, Cork English, Belfast English — all of them on display in *Rhapsody in Stephen's Green*. But he lacked another essential skill, that of constructing and sustaining a plot and theme. 'All words and no play makes Faustus Kelly a dull boyo,' Joseph Holloway complained in his diary, citing a reviewer's demand that Myles 'learn the craft of playwriting'. Holloway's dramatic theories were old-fashioned, but he did recognize that Myles's talent was for the episodic. This may be an occupational hazard of the daily columnist, as Patrick Kavanagh once suggested.[6] Flann O'Brien's novels are highly episodic, especially *At Swim-Two-Birds*, which constantly interrupts and interrogates its own narrative and procedures. *The Third Policeman* is an extended metaphysical joke in which nothing happens, nothing can happen, because time, and therefore narrative, have ceased. Given this tendency toward the episodic, it is not surprising that the brief *Thirst* was Myles's most successful play, set, as it is, out of time, in a country pub after time has ended — that is, after the legal closing hour, once signalled by the barman's cry, 'Time, please, gents.' The play's action, or rather talk, occurs in a pub whose proprietor pretends he is not serving drinks to drinkers who pretend they are not drinking. The play begins with idle bar talk and then becomes a study in the power of language, when the publican describes desert heat and thirst so graphically that the Sergeant, arriving to enforce the law, must himself break the law by drinking the proffered pints.

Faustus Kelly starts well, with a dumb show prologue in which Kelly sells his soul to the devil, in return, we later learn, for election to the Dáil and success with the widowed Mrs Crockett. Act I works because it is all talk, the meeting of a County Council and the interplay among its members: the wheedling Shawn Kilshaughran, the oleaginous Cullen, the cantankerous Reilly, even the silent Hoop. Myles displays his skill at Irish local accents with Kilshaughran's 'thick western brogue', the Town Clerk's 'strong Cork accent', and Hoop's 'pronounced Northern accent'. But Act II introduces a new character and new issues

6

insufficiently connected with those of Act I; III meanders, to end feebly with the devil tearing up the contract Kelly had signed and vowing to have nothing more to do with Irish politicians. The play also suffers from Kelly's tendency to address everyone as if he or she were a public meeting, in long turgid election speeches — good enough parodies of contemporary political oratory, no doubt, but tedious rather than amusing. When the devil tears up the contract, we suspect it may be because he realized how boring Hell would be with Faustus Kelly in it.

Rhapsody in Stephen's Green succeeds because it does not depend on sustaining a plot or theme. It is appropriately episodic, each act coming to its own resolution, and is in fact a series of one-act plays. Myles did not need to contrive a plot or devise a way to sustain it. He had only to adapt the episodic structure of the Čapek brothers' Czech original.[7] But despite owing its concept, structure, and some incidents to the Čapeks, *Rhapsody in Stephen's Green* is essentially an original work by Myles himself. The critical failure of *Faustus Kelly* may have made this man of many identities look for yet another. Like the poet James Clarence Mangan (1803-49), who often protected himself by describing his own poems as translations from the German, the Hebrew, the Ottoman, Myles may have decided to protect himself by offering Dublin his own version of a play that had succeeded in London and New York — or rather, his own improvization upon aspects of that play.

The original *Insect Play*, in Czech *Ze života hmyzu* (1921), literally 'from the life of insects', was written by Karel Čapek (1890-1938), like Myles a novelist and journalist as well as playwright. His collaborator was his brother, Josef Čapek (1887-1945). The first performances were at Brno (3 February 1922) and Prague (8 April 1922).[8] Adapted as *The World We Live In*, by Owen Davis, the play ran for 111 performances at the Jolson Theatre, New York, opening on 31 October 1922. A London production soon followed, at the Regent Theatre (5 May 1923; 42 performances), this time in Paul Selver's translation, very freely adapted by Nigel Playfair and Clifford Bax.[9] At the Regent, a very young John Gielgud played an effete poet-butterfly, Elsa Lanchester was a voracious Larva, and Synge's beloved Maire O'Neill, who had created the roles of his Pegeen Mike and Deirdre at the Abbey, was Mrs Beetle.

7

Karel Čapek was the first Czech author since Comenius to achieve a reputation outside his own country, largely due to his play *R.U.R. (Rossum's Universal Robots)* (1920), within five years translated into German, Slovenian, Hungarian, English, Japanese, French, and Russian.[10] *R.U.R.*, translated by Selver, opened in London in April 1923, for 126 performances, adding a concept and a word — robot — to the English language. Čapek's play imagines the invention of 'Rossum's Universal Robots' (the phrase is in English in the Czech original), who take over most of the world's work, but eventually rebel and destroy their human masters. Many later works of science fiction have repeated Čapek's apocalyptic vision of man destroyed by his own machines. But Čapek made a subtler point. His robots rebel when they have been made so human as to think and feel, and recognize their own status as slaves. Čapek's real target was the dehumanization of human workers in the new world of assembly lines and efficiency experts. At about the time he wrote, Henry Ford's autobiography, H.N. Casson's *Axioms of Business*, and several similar works advocating 'efficiency' appeared in Czech translation, among them *Principles of Scientific Management* (1911; *Základy vědeckého vedení*, Prague 1925) by Frederick Winslow Taylor (1856-1915), the inventor of the time-motion study. Taylor's ideas are parodied in *R.U.R.* and again in Act III of *Rhapsody*.[11]

The chief source for *The Insect Play*, as Karel Čapek acknowledged, was *La vie des insectes* (1910), extracts from the ten-volume *Souvenirs entomologiques* (1879-1907) by the French entomologist Jean-Henri Fabre (1823-1915). Fabre describes the activities of various insects, including those who figure in the play, in language that continually invites us to compare them with humans:

> Once his ball is ready, a dung-beetle issues from the crowd and leaves the work-yard, pushing his spoil behind him. A neighbour, one of the newcomers, whose own task is hardly begun, suddenly drops his work and runs to the ball now rolling, to lend a hand· to the lucky owner, who seems to accept the proffered aid kindly. Henceforth, the two cronies work as partners. Each does his best to push the pellet to a place of safety. Was a compact really concluded in the work-

yard, a tacit agreement to share the cake between them? . . .
The eager fellow-worker, under the deceitful pretence of
lending a helpful hand, nurses the scheme of purloining the
ball at the first opportunity . . . I ask myself in vain what
Proudhon introduced into Beetle-morality the daring para-
dox that 'property is based on plunder', or what diplomatist
taught Dung-beetles the savage maxim that 'might is right'.[12]

Myles's explicit reference to St Stephen's Green emphasizes his
intention to localize the play in Dublin, to make it Irish and his
own. The freedom with which he treated the Čapeks' text, at times
ignoring it completely, resembles his sometimes parodic, sometimes creative, use of the Old Irish *Buile Suibhne* in *At Swim-Two-
Birds*.

The Čapek Brothers published a 'comedy in three acts, with
prologue and epilogue'. In their Prologue, a Pedant who collects
butterflies encounters a Tramp who soliloquizes, partly in blank
verse. The Tramp suffers from some metaphysical sorrow. He has
fought in the Great War, and emerged, if not shell-shocked, disil-
lusioned. A man, but also Man, he meditates aloud on the Pedant's claim that Nature is eternal mating. Myles's Scene 1 elimi-
nates the Pedant, and is a little Dublin vignette of bullying, official, social, and linguistic, as a Grounds Keeper with a strong
Dublin accent aggressively clears St Stephen's Green at closing
time. He is intimidated by a well-dressed lounger who claims —
in a 'very "cultured"' accent — to be an important official, threat-
ens retaliation, and reduces the Keeper to abject pleading. The
Tramp, with an even more pronounced Dublin accent, appears
only at the end of the Prologue, commenting on the presence of
bees. Myles's Prologue has little to do with the rest of the play,
apart from introducing the Tramp and clearing Stephen's Green
of all but one of its human inhabitants.

The Čapeks' Act I is about butterflies. Myles's is about bees. The
Čapek butterflies are bright young things, children of the jazz age,
the females literally flappers. Bored, languid, promiscuous, they
haunt an elegant little cocktail-bar, where the timid and yearning
Felix (Gielgud's 1923 role) pursues Iris (*Apatura iris*, the purple
emperor) with sentimental verses, but fails to recognize her sexual
eagerness. Myles's bees are even more enervated, and discuss

9

suicide in Trinity accents. A Drone recites passages from Shakespeare, the closest Myles gets to Felix's poetic effusions. The Queen Bee seeks in vain to mate. The Tramp is stung.

Myles follows the Čapeks — or rather, their English translator — a little more closely in Acts II and III. But where the Čapeks introduce a moth Chrysalis eager to be born, Myles gives us a hen's talking Egg. The Čapeks' Ichneumon Fly (*Ichneumonidae*) and its Larva become a Duck and Duckling. Myles retains the Brothers' Dung-beetles, male and female, giving them 'appalling' Dublin accents and more strongly emphasizing their greedy petty capitalism. He also retains their Crickets, here with Cork accents. The Beetles' preoccupation with their ball of dung, and the Crickets' preoccupation with her pregnancy and their search for a new house, are repeated in Myles's text, though putting Mr Cricket 'in de [Civil] service' is his addition. He also retains the Parasite, who agrees with everyone; 'the last word in mealy-mouthed joxers', he may owe something to Sean O'Casey's 'Joxer' Daly.

In Act III, Myles's chief innovation is to make some Ants Northern Unionists, who speak with strong Belfast accents. They are determined to defend their 'holy ralugion' against the 'dirty Green Awnts' of the South, who obey 'thon awnt over in Rome' and force 'the wee awnts' to learn Latin, 'a dad longuage'. Myles keeps the Čapeks' satire against assembly lines and efficiency experts, and ends the act, as they do, with a savage war — in which red or British ants also attack the Unionists. When the Red Ant demands military assistance and supplies from the Orange Ants, Myles is hinting to his audience that the British were making similar demands on the Irish government. The Orange Ants' refusal provokes an invasion by Red and Green Ants in alliance — a reversal of the real possibility in 1943, Ireland's well-founded fear of a British invasion, which would have included Northern Irish units. Myles was able to get this past the vigilant censors, perhaps because of its sheer audacity — to end with a thinly disguised Eamon de Valera, master of all he survives, proclaiming himself Emperor of the World in Irish. As in the Čapek original, the Tramp, disgusted by the triumphant Emperor, crushes him.

'Gob, I never seen so many children', Myles's final line, acknowledges without endorsing the 'life goes on' theme of the

Capeks' sentimental epilogue. In Myles's epilogue, the theme is a general indifference to the Tramp's death. The children we see, and those the courting couple plan to have, offer little reason for optimism.

Despite Myles's popularity and verbal ingenuity, *The Insect Play* was not a great success at the Gaiety, playing only for a week. Though the playwright came to believe that some sort of conspiracy had been mounted against him, perhaps because his satire seemed aimed at specific individuals,[13] reviewers for his own paper and for the *Irish Independent* were enthusiastic. The unsigned *Irish Times* review (probably by Brinsley MacNamara) noted that Myles 'has taken away a good deal from the version through which we had come to know' the play, 'and added a great deal that is his own . . . he makes it rather more of an entertainment.' But the 'depths' are still there, and the target, human selfishness and pride, is Swift's target: 'Swift's version of Lilliput is not so very different from what the sleeping tramp . . . sees in Stephen's Green.' *The Irish Times* recognized in the Tramp the 'Chorus who represents us', and approved the local setting:

> There was a familiarity . . . about some of the bees, beetles, crickets, ducks and ants that left us in no doubt of the part of the world we were looking at through the eyes of the Tramp. There were moments when they brought us quite close to topics of the day, when we were as near to certain things as some of those things now are to Stephen's Green.[14]

The *Irish Independent* was even more enthusiastic ('an enjoyable satire'), especially about the local setting, seeing 'no artistic reason' to prefer Prague over Dublin, 'or why the tramp should not speak in the adenoidal whine of Dublin and in its breezy, if adjectively limited, vernacular . . . With the social satire cleverly adapted to our own problems I feel we saw the play as the brothers Capek would have like their own nationalists to see it.'[15]

Joseph Holloway, usually so difficult to please, was nearing the end of his long career as a Dublin playgoer — he died in March 1944. Holloway was present as usual on opening night. 'Loud applause followed the fall of the curtain,' he noted, 'but I fear Myles had strayed miles away from the Čapeks' play and its import. As we saw it . . . it was just a pointless burlesque in Irish dialect over-emphasized to the point of grotesque exaggeration.' Holloway liked MacLiammóir's costumes, the bees, and the mechanical movements of the ants, which he compared to those of the animated cartoons featuring Felix the Cat. But he condemned Myles's demotic language:

> The adaptor had turned the play into Stage-Irish dialect, of many counties, and introduced far too many 'bloodies' and 'Ah gods' into his text. Much of the talk reminded me of the good old red-nosed [word illegible] apelike music hall Irish cross-talkers of long ago! I am sure that the play is interesting and often touching in the original form. As we saw it at the Gaiety it was a thing of sheer burlesque and in the ants scene the Irish were held up to ridicule in cruelly crude fashion, though the scene was wonderfully conveyed . . . and the warring among the ants cleverly done.[16]

A few days later, Holloway complained again about the frequent appearance of the word 'bloody', quoting the Gate actor Michael J. Dolan, who had told Myles 'that the repeated use of the word only shewed the poverty of his expression', and adding, 'I heard that his adaptation of *The Insect Play* was a flop at the Gaiety. His stage efforts are distinctly vulgar and common, and not suitable in the Gaiety, the Abbey, or the Gate.'[17]

T.W. of the *Irish Press* was even less complimentary, giving the play a dismissive 'interesting', but then moving to the attack: 'I am still wondering if William Shakespeare, the Czech brothers Čapek, and Myles na gCopaleen, with a dash of Jimmy O'Dea and Harry O'Donovan, is a digestible dish.' T.W. noted Myles's 'remarkable and close intimacy with the vernacular of the public hostelries of this ancient capital,' wondered why people laughed at the word 'bloody,' and defended the Čapeks against their adaptor: 'an author who depends on phony bravado like this is offering a poor substitute for drama.' The Čapeks, he insisted,

> wrote a serious satire on the cruelties of the world . . . They would have been surprised to find their cornerstone being used . . . to burlesque the divisions in this country to make a theatrical holiday.
>
> The Čapeks, lovers of their country, would have been amazed to find their translator and adaptor using their work

to mock the movement for reviving a national language and to sneer at the people of Ireland, North and South.

Other parts of the play were in extremely bad taste; cheap jokes about motherhood are not worthy of any civilization.[18]

Writing in the Catholic *Standard*, Gabriel Fallon made similar objections to the play's 'expletives', provoking Myles into calling him 'a wretched pedant'.[19]

The stiffness of the *Irish Press* review suggests a possible paying off of scores for the satire of *An Béal Bocht*. The *Press* was the property of Eamon de Valera, then Taoiseach and easily recognizable as the Irish-speaking leader of the Green Ants. The paper was the organ of the Fianna Fáil party, self-anointed as the guardian of the national language and the national identity. Though the reviewer apparently had some knowledge of the Čapeks' work, he seems to take their play too seriously. A similarity between human and insect life was hardly a new idea in Dublin — the King of Brobdingnag 'was amazed how so impotent and groveling an insect' as Gulliver could be so 'inhuman' and bloodthirsty as to advocate the manufacture and use of gun powder.

Myles's *Rhapsody in Stephen's Green* neither betrays nor misuses its Czech source. It is essentially a new work, local rather than ostentatiously universal, but local as *Ulysses* is local, able to include a broad range of human behaviour. Though the Čapeks left it to the director to decide whether the characters would be people acting like insects, or insects acting like people,[20] Myles is more decisive. He is bleaker, more pitiless. His humans are insects. Beckett's tramps wait in the wings. Myles's bracing Swiftian scorn leaves no room for optimism — except that the scorn is so presented as to provoke laughter, and laughter can be redemptive.

ROBERT TRACY
Berkeley, California

1 See Anne Clissman, *Flann O'Brien: A Critical Introduction to His Writings* (Dublin: Gill and Macmillan, 1975), 22-3; 260-63; and Anthony Cronin, *No Laughing Matter: The Life and Times of Flann O'Brien* (London: Grafton, 1989), 135-6. Act I was published in the *Journal of Irish Literature* 3: 1 (January 1974), 24-39. *Rhapsody in Stephen's Green* was Myles's working title, and the play was so announced until just before opening night, when it was re-christened *The Insect Play*, the usual English title of the Čapeks' play.

2 O'Nolan, O Nualláin on Civil Service lists, served in Dublin in the Department of Local Government (1935-54). In 1937-43 he was Private Secretary to several successive Ministers of Local Government.

3 See Myles na gCopaleen, *The Best of Myles: A Selection from 'Cruiskeen Lawn'*, ed. Kevin O'Nolan (London: MacGibbon and Kee, 1968), 202, 203, 219, 212.

4 Myles na gCopaleen, *Further Cuttings from Cruiskeen Lawn*, ed. Kevin O'Nolan (London: Hart-Davis, MacGibbon, 1976), 137; 95.

5 Flann O'Brien, *Stories and Plays* (London: Hart-Davis, MacGibbon, 1973), 81-89.

6 Joseph Holloway, Manuscript Diaries, National Library of Ireland, MSS 2009, 163. For Kavanagh's comment, see Cronin, 165.

7 'The authors know that their comedy, *From the Life of the Insect World*, is not a real play, a formal play ... it is rather a compilation, consisting of three or four one act plays ... They are somewhat connected by the figure of the Tramp...' Karel Čapek, 'Poznámky k Zivotu hmyzu: Před premiérou v Národním divadle' (Notes on *Life of the Insects*: Before Opening Night at the National Theatrez, *Jeviště* (Stage) 3 (1922); reprinted in Karel Čapek, *Spisy* 18: *O umènia kulture* (On Art and Culture) 2: 398 (Praha: Československý spisovatel, 1985).

8 See Karel Čapek and Josef Čapek, *Ze spolecné tvorby* (From the Collected Works), *Spisy* (Writings) (Praha: Československý spisovatel, 1982), 2: 403.

9 Davis's version is in *Twenty Best European Plays on the American Stage*, ed. John Gassner (New York: Crown Publishers, 1957), 597-695; it was also published by Samuel French (1933). The Selver-Playfair-Bax version appeared in 1923 (Oxford University Press). Selver's more accurate translation is in *International Modern Plays* (London: Dent/ Everyman's Library, 1950).

10 Boris Mědílek a kolektiv, *Bibliografie Karla Čapka* (Praha: Academia, 1990), 466-533.

11 When 2nd Engineer finds 'a new way of mackin' them wurk quacker', by speeding up the count. Čapek notes the presence of 'the idea of Taylorism' (*myšlenku taylorismu*) in 'Poznámky k Zivotu hmyzu', *Spisy* 18: 397.

12 Fabre, Jean-Henry, *The Life and Love of the Insect*, trans. Alexander Teixeira de Mattos (London: A. and C. Black, 1911), 8-11. Karel Čapek acknowledges his debt to Fabre in 'Poznámky k Zivotu hmyzu, *Spisy* 18: 397.

13 Cronin, 135; Peter Costello and Peter Van de Camp, *Flann O'Brien: An Illustrated Biography* (London: Bloomsbury, 1987), 82.

14 *The Irish Times* 22 March 1943: 3. For MacNamara's authorship, see Costello/Van de Camp 82.

15 *Irish Independent* 23 March 1943: 6.

16 Holloway, Manuscript Diaries, National Library of Ireland, MSS 2009, 519-20.

17 Joseph Holloway, *Joseph Holloway's Irish Theatre*, ed. Robert Hogan and Michael J. O'Neill (Dixon, California: Proscenium Press, 1970), 3 (1938-1944), 86.

18 *Irish Press* 23 March 1943: p. 3 col. 4.

19 *Further Cuttings* 169. Myles and Fallon exchanged shots in *The Standard* (2 April 1943). S.M. Dunn may be another mask for the playwright:

> Our Theatre Critic Attacked and Defended
>
> Letter from Myles na gCopaleen:
>
> Dear Sir,—Last week you were good enough to publish an article by Gabriel Fallon in which it was suggested that myself and about 150 other people were engaged in presenting obscenities and salacities on the Dublin stage. I must, therefore, ask you to publish this letter.
>
> Myself and the other people concerned are content to endure the implication that as Christians and Catholics we are very inferior to Mr. Fallon. We claim, however, a sense of aesthetic delicacy, and we protest very strongly against a dirty tirade which, under the guise of dramatic criticism, was nothing more or less than a treatise on dung. 'There will always be a distinction,' Mr. Fallon says, 'between the honest dung of the farmyard and the nasty dirt of the chicken run.' Personally I lack the latrine erudition to comment on this extraordinary statement, and I am not going to speculate on the odd researches that led your contributor to his great discovery. I am content to record my objection that his faecal reveries should be published.
>
> This second point I want to make clear to your readers is that *there is no foundation whatsoever* for Mr. Fallon's statements that the 'Insect Play' abounded in obscenity, filthy language, and gibes at sacred things. The three things mentioned specifically by Mr. Fallon are sex, motherhood, and *double entendre*. There is no reference to sex as such anywhere; it is true that there are male and female characters, but very few people nowadays consider that alone an indelicacy. There is a pathetic and beautiful passage where a cricket who is going to have a baby is murdered; as a modest part-author I am in position to call this pathetic and beautiful because the scene is Čapek verbatim. Your wretched pedant has never read or seen Čapek's play. As to *double entendre*, there is not a single example of this objectionable music-hall device in the piece from first to last. The entire play is a salutary *double entendre* and may well present to the mentally adolescent the same sort of shock that was given by the Rouault picture [of Christ], which was denounced as blasphemous by many responsible persons and is now housed in St Patrick's College, Maynooth. That your Mr. Fallon is not even educated is evident from the extraordinary stuff he publishes in your paper every week. In the article in question, for instance, with the phraseen *gamin de genie*, he affords your readers a glimpse of the tired European who is not quite at home in English; this impression is more than strengthened when we find the master using the word 'adaption' — twice, unfortunately,

thus letting out the scapegoat printer. I cannot find 'adaption' in any dictionary. It must be French, I suppose.

Here, however, is the main point of this letter. After sending you his disquisition on dung, Mr. Fallon communicated with the Director of the Boy Scouts employed in the play and used every endeavour to make him withdraw the boys so that the whole presentation would be sabotaged; he did not succeed, and presumably an opportunity will be found later for associating the Boy Scout organization with dung, which is Mr. Fallon's symbol of disapproval. Since your paper honours Mr. Fallon with the role of critic, I think he is entitled to denounce every single play he sees if he feels that way about it, however much his disapproval may be the result of ignorance or mental immaturity. That he should take steps to close down a show he does not like is, I think, a unique departure in dramatic criticism. When he finds himself excluded as an undesirable from all theatres, as he well may, he will have to find some other rostrum from which to direct his foul-mouthed campaign for decency and reticence.

THE TRANSLATOR OF THE INSECT PLAY

Letter from Member of Audience:

Sir—I wish to congratulate you on your article censuring the Gaiety 'Insect Play' last week. In company with a Protestant friend, I visited the show and felt most uncomfortable during the first act. I muttered to my friend: 'This is blasphemous and most suggestive' and the answer I received was in the nature of 'Evil to him who evil thinks'! References to the 'Queen' up in the sky and 'keeping pure till we meet her' made me squirm and the language and use of the Holy Name, along with the 'maternity' act in the second part, was vile.

A lady behind me roared laughing (to put it mildly) at these sallies. What was my amazement to read, then, in my programme that the Catholic Boy Scouts of Ireland were in the cast and a Catholic (!) Myles Na gCopaleen was the translator of this low down jibe at all that we, as Catholics, hold dear. One wonders if Catholic Dublin has loyalty to Faith and principles when such a show could take place during Lent in our principal theatre? Was it shamefacedness that prevented the author appearing on the first night at the last curtain, or was it last minute remorse, at any rate Mr. Edwards seemed annoyed and apologized for his non-appearance.

The only other paper that censured this play was the *Herald*. I would have written to the *Independent* but I know it would be useless as the papers think too much of the advertising end of the theatre business to censure their shows.

I think it is time some league was formed to rouse public opinion against the 'taking in vain' of God's name which has become a scandal on the Dublin stage. Unfortunately, Catholic actors are the commonest offenders . . .

Every educated person, Protestant or Catholic, deplores this tendency and desires some change. Can THE STANDARD lead public opinion to demand it? Say a Matt Talbot League for Catholics, for that sainted man never heard the sacred name of Jesus pronounced without lifting his hat, and his dislike of profanity was so great that even though a humble workman his influence was such that bad

16

language came to be unknown in his vicinity.

One occasion was reported of a profaner being faced by Matt Talbot with a crucifix and the words 'Do you know Who you are crucifying?' No more was said and the man hung his head and made no further reply.

s.m. dunn

[Note: In justice to the secular press the *Irish Press*, and to some extent, the *Times Pictorial* joined in the protest against the *Insect Play.*—Editor, the standard.]

Our Theatre Critic's reply and his challenge to Myles na gCopaleen: The translator's letter speaks eloquently for itself.

Not all of its implications can be answered here or at the moment: nevertheless certain important facts must immediately be made clear.

(1) In reference to Paragraph 4 and the letter's 'main point'.

I had no communication whatsoever with the Director of the Boy Scouts concerning this play, nor had I communication with any officer or member of that body concerning it.

(2) As to the reference in Paragraph 3 that *The Standard's* 'wretched pedant' has never read or seen Capek's play —

I have read it; I have seen it; and I have reviewed it as the files of *The Standard* will testify.

So much for the letter, at the moment.

I now challenge the translator of *The Insect Play* to send to the editor of *The Standard* the script of the version played to the audience of the Gaiety Theatre on the evening of Monday, March 22, 1943, in order that the readers of *The Standard* may be convinced of the justice or the injustice of my criticism.

I append a copy of a letter sent by me to the Manager of the Gaiety Theatre on March 25.

My Dear Hamlyn, —In view of last week's presentation by Edwards–MacLiammóir Productions at the Gaiety, I have decided to refrain from attendance at any subsequent presentation which this company may offer during the current season.

I trust that this step, which has been determined after careful consideration, will not in any way interfere with the cordial relations exisiting between *The Standard* Drama Critic and yourself and Mr. Elliman, and the very courteous staff of the Gaiety Theatre.

With every good wish,
Yours Sincerely.
(Signed) Gabriel Fallon.
Hamlyn Benson, Esq., Manager, Gaiety Theatre, Dublin.

20 'Poznamky k Zivotu hmyzu,' *Spisy* 18: 399.

ACKNOWLEDGMENTS

Rhapsody in Stephen's Green survives thanks to the acumen of R. Russell Maylone, Curator of Special Collections, Northwestern University Library, who obtained the Gate Theatre Archive. I am grateful to him, and to Mrs. Evelyn O'Nolan, for permission to publish the play. I also wish to thank Ann Tisa of the Northwestern Library's Special Collections for her help, and Daniel H. Garrison of the Northwestern University Department of Classics for patiently checking many details. My other debts of gratitude are to Sheila Ryan, Curator of Manuscripts at the Morris Library, Southern Illinois University at Carbondale, where Myles's papers are kept; to Nancy Axelrod of the Entomological Library, University of California, Berkeley; to Patricia Donlon, Director of the National Library of Ireland, for permission to quote unpublished passages from Joseph Holloway's diaries; and to Margaret Mc Peake and her Apple Macintosh.

R.T.

Rhapsody in Stephen's Green was first performed (as *The Insect Play*) by the Gate Theatre Company at the Gaiety Theatre, Dublin, on 22 March 1943. The cast was as follows:

THE TRAMP	Robert Hennessy
A LADY IN THE GREEN	Rosalind Halligan
CHILDREN	Tony Mathews, Teddy Lucas, Eileen Ashe, Collette Redmond, Ita McManus, Deirdre King, Dolores Lucas, Peggy Kennedy, Maeve Kennedy
A GIRL STUDENT	Patricia Kennedy
A YOUNG MAN	James Neylin
A VISITOR	Liam Gaffney
THE KEEPER	William Fassbender
THE DRONE BEE	Stephen King
BASIL BEE	Cecil Monson
CECIL BEE	Norman Barrs
CYRIL BEE	Antony Walsh
A YOUNG BEE	Robert Dawson
HER MAJESTY QUEEN BEE	Betty Chancellor
A DUCKLING	Alexis Milne
THE VOICE OF THE EGG	Jean St Clair
THE DUCK	P.P. Maguire
MR BEETLE	William Fassbender
MRS BEETLE	Sally Travers
A STRANGE BEETLE	Tyrell Pine
MR CRICKET	J. Winter
MRS CRICKET	Meriel Moore
A PARASITE	Liam Gaffney
A BLIND ANT	William Fassbender
THE CHIEF ENGINEER ANT	J. Winter
THE 2ND ENGINEER ANT	Sean Colleary
THE POLITICIAN ANT	Antony Walsh
A MESSENGER ANT	Liam Gaffney
A CROSS-CHANNEL ANT	Norman Barrs
SLATTERY	Val Iremonger

GREEN ANTS, RED ANTS, ORANGE ANTS, ANTS OF THE GAEL AND ANTS OF THE PALE.

DIRECTOR/PRODUCER	Hilton Edwards
SETTINGS	Molly MacEwen
COSTUMES	Micheál MacLiammóir

PROLOGUE

St Stephen's Green. Probably near the lake, there is a row of chairs with their backs to the audience; some are deck chairs and some the upright green twopenny type.[1] Most of them are occupied. Dusk is falling (and pretty fast too). The bells of the keepers summoning the visitors to leave are heard in the distance. A few small children rush across the foreground shouting and playing with a ball; they run out again. A bell is heard being banged very loud off. Enter a comic KEEPER carrying the bell. He looks from behind at the row of inert seated figures, his back to the audience. His stance and silence suggest patient disgust. Suddenly he gives a savage ear-splitting clang of the bell, startling everybody, including the audience.

> KEEPER   Do yez know the time or have yez no home to go to?[2]

A very mixed group get up hastily, glare at the KEEPER and move off. A fat lady calls to her children, two old men shamble off muttering, a student and some others leave in the manner that fits them. A very pronounced bulge in the back of one of the deck-chairs at the right-hand side of the row remains, however. The KEEPER eyes it and approaches stealthily. He then gives a really ferocious clang on the bell.

> KEEPER   Will yeh get up to hell ou' a that and clear out of this pairk, d'yeh hear me!

An irate fat well-dressed figure has jumped up out of the chair. His accent is very 'cultured'.

> VISITOR   What the devil do you mean?
> KEEPER   *(Sarcastic in a steely way)* I beg yer pardin?
> VISITOR   How dare you talk to me like that — how dare you ring your bell like that in my ear?
> KEEPER   Now luckit here, don't give me anny trouble. This pairk is closed down be the regulations

from sunset. And all the visitors has to be cleared out, d'yeh understhand me. All has to go off an' leave the premises. It's just like a public house. Come on now, sir, yeh'll have to pack up, yeh'll have all day to-morra to be lying down there snoozin'!

VISITOR   (*Flabbergasted at all this familiarity*) Well upon my word! Who the devil do you think you're speaking to? Of all the . . . infernal . . . nerve!

KEEPER   I don't want anny trouble now, DON'T GIVE ME ANNY TROUBLE. Out yeh'll have to go and that's all about it. It's a very seryus thing to be in the pairk after dairk.

VISITOR   How dare you address members of the public in that impertinent fashion! How dare you set out to injure people's hearing with that bell of yours! HOW DARE YOU SIR!

KEEPER   (*With fake resignation*) Well, of course . . . I dunno. I don't know what I'll do with this man at all. I don't know what I'll do with this man *at all.*

VISITOR   Permit me to remark that it is rather a question of what will be done with you, my man.

KEEPER   (*Mechanical reply to any 'difficult' speech*) I beg yer pardin?

VISITOR   Do you know who I am?

KEEPER   (*Brushing aside a very old story with his flat hand*) Now listen. Luckit here. I don't want to know yer name, yer address, or who yer mother was. Are yeh gettin' out or are yeh not? Now don't tell me I'll have to call a Gaird.[3]

VISITOR   (*Getting ready to leave*) From your offensive behaviour it's rather obvious you don't know who I am but you may learn sooner than you expect.

KEEPER   I don't give a damn if yer de Valera . . . or one of them lads out of the Kildare Street Club[4] . . . or (*tremendous effort*) the Bishop . . . of . . . Bangalore—OUT—OF—THIS—PAIRK—YOU'LL— HAVE—TO GO—AND THAT'S ALL.

VISITOR   Indeed? Perhaps I should tell you who I am.

KEEPER   (*Putting up the hand again to ward off unwanted information*) Now I don't want to hear anny more — I don't want to hear anny more talk or chat at all. This pairk is owned an' run by the Boord of Works,[5] d'yeh understand. And the Boord of Works is a very sthrict crowd . . . a very . . . sthrict . . . crowd.

VISITOR   (*Interested*) Really.

KEEPER   D'yeh undhersthand me now. The Boord has very sthrict regulations for clearin' out the pairk after dairk. I don't care who y'are — all has to pack up and mairch out of the pairk when it gets dairk. It's the Boord's regulations, yeh'll see them pasted up there be the gate.

VISITOR   All this is extremely interesting.

KEEPER   Are yeh gettin' out? Yes or no now.

VISITOR   Extremely interesting.

KEEPER   Because if yer goin' to stop here, I'll go and get a Gaird and it's above in the 'joy[6] yeh'll spend the night, me good man.

VISITOR   If you knew who you are speaking to, you uncouth impudent . . .

KEEPER   (*Almost roaring*) Luckit here, if you were wan of the head buck-cats out of the Board of Works itself, a big offeecial from the place beyant there (*He points*), if you were the head-man in chairge of pairks an' gairdens, I'd mairch you out just the same in double quick time, me bucko!

VISITOR   (*Angry but gloating*) As a matter of fact that's exactly who I am. (*He begins to move off*)

KEEPER   I beg yer pardin?

VISITOR   That's exactly who I am.

KEEPER   (*Dumfounded*) I beg yer pardin?

VISITOR   That's exactly who I am.

KEEPER   (*Exit out after the visitor, making desperate efforts to retrieve the damage*) But I beg yer pardin kindly sir, SHURE I DIDN'T MEAN ANNY HARM, Sir. Didn't I know yeh well an' me only tryin' to

23

take a rise out of yeh, I'd no more think of givin'
guff to yer honour than I would of givin' it to
Mister Connolly,[7] yer honour . . .

They pass out, the VISITOR *very haughty. The light sinks somewhat. Loud
buzzing as if of aeroplanes is heard. The* TRAMP, *who is emaciated
(naturally enough) is concealed in one of the other deck-chairs, making
little or no bulge to betray his presence. The buzzing noise gets louder.
The audience hears the maudlin voice of the hidden* TRAMP. *His accent is
a richer Dublin job than the* KEEPER; *indeed, the latter might be better
with a rich southern New-York-cop intonation.*

TRAMP   Away wid yez now! Away wid yez! Keep offa
me now. (*More buzzing, much nearer*).

TRAMP   Do yez hear me! Get away to hell ou' a that!

*He starts thrashing about with his arms, which betray his location to the
audience. He starts incoherent drunken roaring and falls out of the chair
into full view.*

TRAMP   One sting from one of them lads and begob yeh
could be screwed down in yer coffin in two
days.

*He swipes at invisible bees but carefully preserving his bottle; he pauses
to take a good swig.*

TRAMP   The bee . . . Do you know what I'm goin' to tell
yeh. The bee . . . is one of the worst jobs out.
Them little lads has a bagful of stuff inside them
. . . and they do spend all their time lookin' for
some poor unfortunate omadaun[8] like meself
for to pump it into. Ah yes, a very bad job — the
bee. I don't fancy the bees atchall.

*He swipes madly again and then has a swig. He resumes his monologue
in a very high-pitched confidential voice.*

TRAMP   (*To audience*) I'll tell yez a good wan. I seen a
man — a perrsonal friend of me own — stung be
a bee and him lying on his death-bed. A man
that was given up be the clergy, the docthors,
the nurses, and begob even be the parties that

was to benefit under the will. That's a quare one! Yer man is breathin' his last gasp when the bee flies in and given him pfffff——, a dart in the neck. And do you know what happens? (*He pauses impressively and takes another long suck*) Do you know what happens? Now you won't believe this, as sure as God you'll tell me I'm a liar ... (*Again he pauses for effect and takes another drink*) I'll tell you what happens. Your man ... sits up ... in bed ... and says he: Will one of youz hand me me trousers there ... plee-ez. Ah? That's ... a quare wan for yez. Would yeh believe that? (*He drinks again, somewhat astonished at the anecdote himself*) An' from that good day to this, yer man never looked back and never ever a day's sickness in the bed. D'yeh undhersthand what I'm tellin' yeh? D'yeh undhersthand me now? A very ferocious ... baste, the bee. A very ... contentious ... intimidatin' ... exacerbatin' animal, the bee. But a great man for suckin' honey an' workin' away inside in the nest. Very hard-workin' industrious men, the bees. (*He looks round. There is loud buzzing.*) And d'yeh know what I'm goin' to tell yeh, there's a bloody nest of the buggers around here somewhere. (*He swipes.*) Gou-a-that! Gou'athat to hell away from me, yez black an' yalla own-shucks![9] (*He takes a long drink.*) Begob d'yeh know what it is, yeh can't bate d'ould bottle! I declare to me God I'd be a dead man only for this little drop o' malt,[10] because I have a very heavy cold on me and that's the God's truth. I'm not in me right health. What a man like me wants is ... family allowances, yeh know ... family allowances ... and plenty of free insurance, d'yeh undhersthand me. (*He is becoming more and more maudlin.*) An' house-buildin' facilities for gettin' married, d'yeh know. An' ... wan more cow ... wan more sow . . . an' wan . . . more . . . acre . . . undher th'plough.[11] D'yeh undhersthand me now? D'yeh undhershand what I'm sayin'? Ah yes. Certaintly. Certaintly . . . Certaintly.

He sits down, drinks, sighs, and yawns and drinks. His fading senses are reflected in the sinking light. He lies down finally and is asleep by the time the light is nearly gone.

CURTAIN

ACT I

There is very loud buzzing. Coloured lights reveal in unearthly prettiness the same corner of Stephen's Green.

The bee females are distinguished by high-heeled shoes, coloured handkerchiefs round the head, and various touches of daintiness about the person.

To one side an enormous flower is growing. The bowl of it must be big enough and strong enough for the bees to climb into it and disappear.

Soft ballet music. A young female bee dances in, flits about the stage, looks at the sleeping TRAMP *without much attention, and dances out again. Enter immediately* THE DRONE. *He is the peppery colonel type, gross and debauched, and bent nearly double from sheer laziness. He waddles very slowly so as to reduce to the minimum the fatigue of locomotion. He collapses into one of the deck-chairs, which are now facing audience. Before he collapses, however, he makes a speech.*

> DRONE This castle hath a pleasant seat; the air
> Nimbly and sweetly recommends itself
> Unto our gentle senses.[1]

He falls into the chair and seems to go to sleep. Enter a young bee, BASIL, *very refined in deportment. He starts, seeing* THE DRONE *asleep beside the attractive flower.*

> BASIL Aoh. (*He approaches* THE DRONE, *examines him and then pokes him gently in the ribs.*) I say . . . hallao!
> DRONE (*Without rising or moving, in a graveyard voice*)
> What early tongue so sweet saluteth me?
> Young son, it argues a distemper'd head
> So soon to bid good morrow to thy bed:
> Care keeps his watch in every old man's eye,
> And where care lodges sleep will never lie;
> But where unbruiséd youth with unstuff'd brain
> Doth couch his limbs, there golden sleep doth
>   reign:
> Therefore thy earliness doth me assure

27

	Thou art up-roused by some distemperature.[2]
BASIL	I say aold chap — really! I'm out looking for a spot of honey. Work, you know, and all that. Frightful bore but one has to, you knaow. Grim shaow, working.

THE DRONE is asleep again. BASIL climbs into the flower and disappears. Enter two more bees, somewhat casually. They are CYRIL and CECIL.

CYRIL	I say, Cec-eel, do look at that old rotter. Always asleep I mean.
CECIL	I agree, Cyr-eel, a grey shaow. D'you knaow, there are some people who . . . simply . . . waon't . . . work. (*He approaches flower as if to enter; looks into it and then starts back.*) Ao, bother! That sod Bas-eel!
CYRIL	Is that dreadful Bas-eel working there?
CECIL	Rather. (*He sits down disconsolately.*)
CYRIL	I say, Cec-eel . . .
CECIL	Yes old boy?
CYRIL	D'you mind if I talk to you?
CECIL	Nao, nao.
CYRIL	I mean, are you ever bored by . . . I mean . . . this all-male company idea? I mean, no weemeen.
CECIL	Well, sometimes, you know, I feel . . . I feel . . . I should like to see the Queen.
CYRIL	Ha-ha-ha-ha! (*Mirthless laugh act*)
CECIL	But look here, I mean eet, aold boy.
CYRIL	The Queen!! Ho-ho-ho!
CECIL	(*Seriously*) I should really like to see the Queen. Just for a short time, you knaow. And alone.
CYRIL	One moment now Cec-eel. How many of us bees are there? Rough estimate, you knaow, and all that.
CECIL	A million, I suppaose. Two million.
CYRIL	Well there you are, old boy, there eet ees. Two million bees and one Queen. I mean, what chance have you, Cec-eel. You are a nice boy and all that but what chance have you?
CECIL	(*Crestfallen*) None, I suppose.

28

CYRIL   There eet ees. What can we do? What's the point in being alive? What's the point in all this working?

CECIL   (*Brightly*) Well, I don't know . . . I do think, you knaow . . . that life is rather . . . wizard. Planning and working, I mean. Ambition and all that.

CYRIL   (*Impatiently*) I knaow, but wot . . . ees . . . the point . . . of eet all? Why, why, why? Where ees eet all leading? You do make me tired, Cec-eel.

CECIL   I do think that life is . . . you knaow . . . fine, nobeel, something to live bravely, I mean.

CYRIL   Cec-eel, I do wish you would be quiet, I mean. Wot can we do, WOT CAN WE DO?

CECIL   (*Again brightly*) I will tell you, Cyr-eel. We can STING! We can STING, old boy.

CYRIL   I knaow, I knaow. It is nice, I suppaose. Actually I suppaose eet ees unbearably nice. But the penalty . . . Death, I mean, and all that.

CECIL   (*Grandly*) I am not afraid to die, Cyr-eel.

CYRIL   I knaow. But one sting and we are dead. Is eet worth it, I mean?

CECIL   Cyr-eel, I believe eet ees.

CYRIL   (*Meditatively*) I suppaose you're right, you knaow.

CECIL   (*Eagerly*) I have talked with dying bees just after they have given somebody a sting. And d'you knaow wot they told me?

CYRIL   Wot was eet, old boy?

CECIL   When they were dying, you knaow, they said they heard voices . . . beautiful choirs, you knaow, and the soft music of harps and all that. I do think that to die from giving our sting is to become a martyr. And d'you knaow another thing they told me?

CYRIL   Wot?

CECIL   Absolutely no pain, old boy. They felt as if they were lying in the cups of daffodils, just falling asleep on something soft and sweet. I do think death can be rather charming, you knaow.

CYRIL   I often wondered, Cec-eel — wot ees eet makes us sting. I mean, why do we do eet?

CECIL   Health, old boy. High spirits, you knaow, *joie de vivre* and so on. When a bee is young and healthy and bulging with honey, he simply can't help himself. He ... simply ... can't ... help himself. Stinging may be immoral but really I am sure it must be very nice. Matter of fact, I think I'll soon do a spot of stinging myself.

CYRIL   O, Cec-eel! And die?

CECIL   Well, we all have to die sometime.

CYRIL   I knaow, but still ... Death is a grey grim shaow, you knaow, a grey grim shaow.

CECIL   There is really only one thing that stops me from stinging somebody, Cyr-eel.

CYRIL   And wot is that?

CECIL   The Queen! The hope that one day ... I may meet the Queen ... and marry her, you knaow, old boy, at an altitude of eight hundred thousand feet.[3] Alone, I mean, quite alone, you knaow, in the sky.

CYRIL   I say, Cec-eel, you are silly. A chance of two million to one.

CECIL   But listen, Cyr-eel, d'you knaow that man person that one sees ... ?

CYRIL   That one stings, you mean? (*They laugh.*)

CECIL   Quite. Well I do believe they sell each other little tickets.[4] Tickets for a price, you knaow. Sometimes they sell two million of these tickets.

CYRIL   And wot happens?

CECIL   Why, some blighter wins the prize, of course!

CYRIL   Is that any reason why we should be so foolish, old boy?

CECIL   Well, I daon't knaow. I do think life is very baffling. I mean, what is one to do. Sting, or live on in the hope of meeting the Queen?

CYRIL   Yes, old boy, that's the difficulty. The choice between the sensuous delight of stinging with the rather charming death that follows, or

	keeping oneself ... you knaow ... chaste and alive in the hope of meeting the Queen..It is very difficult, Cec-eel. Very, very difficult.
CECIL	I do think I'll sting some man person, Cyr-eel.
CYRIL	Do wait a little longer, old boy. Control of the passions and all that. One mustn't give in to every impulse, I mean.
CECIL	(*Impatiently*) But really, life is such a bore. It is such a bore being good!
CYRIL	Yes, I knaow. (*He rubs his hands briskly.*) If only one could work, if only Bas-eel would come out of that flower —

There is a violent interruption. A very young and agile bee rushes in, beside himself with hysteria and delight.

| YOUNG BEE | I've done it! I've done it! Ooooooooooh! |
| CYRIL | Wot's all this row? |

The YOUNG BEE *rushes about laughing hysterically but his antics soon weaken; eventually he becomes quiet and sinks down and dies in agony.*

YOUNG BEE	I stung a man, I stung a man! I stung him, I tell you ! Oooooooooooooh!
CECIL	Grim shaow. He's dying, you knaow.
BASIL	(*Putting his head out of the flower*) Do tell me, wot's all this row?
CYRIL	Our friend has shot his bolt. Looks quite young too, I don't knaow wot the country is coming to.
BASIL	Ao. (*He climbs out of the flower carrying a little yellow bag marked 'honey'. This he inadvertently leaves within reach of* THE DRONE, *who is already stirring from the noise.*) I say, he is rather a rotter to be doing that at his age.
CECIL	A grey tragic shaow.
BASIL	'O Death, where is thy sting.' (*All laugh*)[5]
DRONE	(*Awake*)
	Foul whisperings are abroad. Unnatural deeds Do breed unnatural troubles: infected minds To their deaf pillows will discharge their secrets.[6]
BASIL	(*To* THE DRONE) I say old boy, do shut up. (*He*

examines corpse.) I do think this mess should be put away. One should really arrange to die at home, you knaow.

Exit dragging the corpse. THE DRONE *quietly snaffles the bag of honey and begins to consume it covertly.* CYRIL *and* CECIL *are depressed and nervous after the death scene.*

CECIL   (*Hysterically*) Cyr-eel, I do wish I was dead!

CYRIL   I feel like stinging somebody myself now. Why should he have all the fun?

CECIL   Yes, why?

CYRIL   But Cec-eel, I could not bear to part with you. We must die together, you knaow. Suicide pact and all that. We will meet again in a better land.

CECIL   (*Taken aback*) Aoh.

DRONE   (*Feeding contentedly*)
This is the state of the bee; today he puts forth
The tender leaves of hope; tomorrow blossoms
And bears his blushing honours thick upon him;
The third day comes a frost, a killing frost,
And — when he thinks, good easy bee, full surely
His greatness is a-ripening — nips his root,
And then he falls . . . [7]

CECIL   (*Annoyed*) I say, do shut up, you awful useless parasite!

CYRIL   Yes, do be quiet, you fat good-for-nothing sponger!

DRONE   (*Unabashed*) If I am
Traduced by ignorant tongues, which neither know
My faculties nor person, yet will be
The chronicles of my doing, let me say
'Tis but the fate of place, and the rough brake
That virtue must go through.[8]

CECIL   (*Shouting*) I say, if you don't keep quiet I shall tumble you out of that chair and kick the head off you!

CYRIL	Oh, the bastard! (*They turn their backs on him.*)
CECIL	Cyr-eel.
CYRIL	Yes, old boy.
CECIL	D'you really think we should die, disappear forever from this earth and all that?
CYRIL	I really believe I do, old boy. I mean, if we go on living, we will have to go on working. Like Bas-eel there, you know. And I do think, Cec-eel, that there is absolutely no point in working. Working makes one vulgar, you knaow. And I am absolutely sick of the sight of honey. I mean, all that yellow mess.
CECIL	By Jove I think you're right, I think you've got eet. Why work? Why work for nothing? I mean, what do we get out of it?
CYRIL	One chance in two million of having ten minutes with the Queen at eight hundred thousand feet. Not worth eet, old boy, definitely not worth eet.
CECIL	Rather not.
CYRIL	Shall we die, Cec-eel? Shall we sting? Shall we have just one glorious . . . marvellous . . . sting?
CECIL	Together, old boy?
CYRIL	Of course. We must both die at the same time. We must make a pact, you knaow. . .
DRONE	Things done well, And with a care, exempt themselves from fear; Things done without example, in their issue Are to be feared. Have you a precedent Of this commission? I believe, not any.[9]
CECIL	That settles eet! I do think I would die without even stinging if I had to listen to more of that rotter's dreadful talk. I say Cyr-eel, do let us die.
CYRIL	But how, old boy? I mean, if I sting somebody and die, how can I be sure that you will do the same? Fair is fair, you knaow, old boy.
CECIL	That is a point, isn't it.
CYRIL	It ees a point, you knaow. (*They think.*)
CECIL	(*Excitedly*) I say! I've got eet! I've got eet! We

	have to sting to die? Right?
CYRIL	RIGHT.
CECIL	We want to die together?
CYRIL	Right.
CECIL	Therefore we must sting together?
CYRIL	Right.
CECIL	Therefore we must sting EACH OTHER!
CYRIL	Right. RIGHT!
CECIL	So there you are, there eet ees. Simple, isn't it?
CYRIL	Deucedly simple, old boy. (*Pause*)
CECIL	Shall we do eet now, Cyr-eel?
CYRIL	(*Reluctantly*) I suppose we should, Cec-eel. I suppose we should, really.
CECIL	(*Resolutely*) Well, let's.

They approach each other gingerly. THE DRONE *is half asleep and pays absolutely no attention.* CECIL *and* CYRIL *timidly shake hands.*

CYRIL	Well . . . old boy . . . eet has been nice knaowing you.
CECIL	Pleasure all mine, old chap.
CYRIL	Sorry to part and all that.
CECIL	It does frightfully depress one, I mean. Fearful grey shaow.
CYRIL	But we will meet again in a better land and all that, don't you think?
CECIL	Ao, rather. And where every bee will have a queen to himself, one hopes.
CYRIL	I say, that *is* an idea. One hopes eet ees true, you knaow.
CECIL	One definitely does, I mean.
CYRIL	Well, old chap . . . so long!
CECIL	Cheers, Cyr-eel, old boy.

They turn back to back suddenly and bump their bums together. Immediately they are galvanized into frenzied prancing and screaming; they die like the YOUNG BEE *earlier.* THE DRONE *looks on, bored.*

DRONE	What should this mean? What sudden anger's this? How have they reap'd it?

34

They parted frowning from me, as if ruin
Leap'd from their eyes: so looks the chaféd lion
Upon the daring huntsman that has gall'd him;
Then makes him nothing. Nay then, farewell!
They've touched the highest point of all their
    greatness;
And, from that full meridian of their glory,
They haste now to their setting; they shall fall
Like a bright exhalation in the evening,
And no bee see them more.[10]

Soft martial music is heard off; the lights change, presaging something momentous. THE DRONE *resumes his honeyed doze. Alone,* THE QUEEN *of all the bees enters. For glitter and majesty she must exceed even Meriel Moore as the courtesan in 'Jack-in-the-Box'.[11]* THE QUEEN *must be a superlatively erotic job.*

QUEEN   What! More dead bees! (*She is horrified.*) Aoh!
        Am I left alone . . . with no bee at all . . . after
        ignoring two million of them . . . for years and
        years . . . ?
DRONE   (*Stirring in his sleep*)
        Who's there, I say? How dare you thrust your-
            selves
        Into my private meditations?[12]
QUEEN   What! Is this alive? How dare you? (*She ap-
        proaches and examines the sleeping* DRONE; *her dis-
        gust is tempered by the fact that after all he is alive
        and a male.*) Aoh.
DRONE   (*Asleep*) I prithee, go to.[13]
QUEEN   Aoh, the nasty old man!
DRONE   (*Asleep*)
        In peace there's nothing so becomes a man
        As modest stillness and humility;
        But, when the blast of war blows in our ears,
        Then imitate the action of the tiger;
        Stiffen the sinews, summon up the blood;
        Disguise fair nature with hard-favour'd rage:
        Then lend the eye a terrible aspect;
        Let it pry through the portage of the head

35

Like the brass cannon; let the brow o'erwhelm it
As fearfully as doth a gallèd rock
O'erhang and jutty his confounded base
Swill'd with the wild and wasteful ocean.
Now set the teeth, and stretch the nostril wide;
Hold hard the breath, and bend up every spirit
To his full height!¹⁴

QUEEN   Aoh!

DRONE   Let us seek some desolate shade, and there
Weep our sad bosoms empty.¹⁵

QUEEN   (Incensed) The wretch is drunk with honey! Of
all the nerve! How dare the wretch treat his
Queen like this — the only female bee in the
whole country! How dare he!

DRONE   Like the Pontick sea,
Whose icy current and compulsive course
Ne'er feels retiring ebb, but keeps due on
To the Propontic and the Hellespont;
Even so my *bloody* thoughts, with violent pace,
Shall ne'er look back, ne'er ebb to humble love,
Till that capable and wide revenge
Swallow them up.¹⁶

QUEEN   (Rushing over and shaking him) You miserable sot!
How dare you mumble your drunken rubbish
in the presence of your Queen! HOW DARE
YOU! Wake up! Do you hear me? WAKE UP! I
command you to wake up, you drunken scoundrel. I am the Queen! THE QUEEN!

DRONE   (Only half-waking)
This argues fruitfulness and liberal heart,
Hot, hot, and moist! This hand of yours requires
A sequester from liberty, fasting and prayer,
Much castigation, exercise devout . . . ¹⁷

QUEEN   Wake up! Do you hear me? I command you —
WAKE UP! You are the last living bee and I
command you to marry me! Do you hear? I
COMMAND YOU TO MARRY ME!

DRONE   Where, where, where?

QUEEN   (Pointing up) Up there, eight hundred thousand

	feet up — you know very well where. WAKE UP, you miserable sot! Do you want the race to die out, you cynical nincompoop? WAKE UP!
DRONE	(*Half-awake*) Stay, my pet, And let your reason with your choler question What 'tis you go about. To climb steep hills Requires slow pace at first: anger is like A full-hot horse, who being allow'd his way, Self-mettle tires him.[18]
QUEEN	(*Mad*) Do you refuse? You disobey me? You disobey your Queen's command? YOU REFUSE TO MARRY ME, YOU TREASONABLE SCOUNDREL! (*She cries hysterically.*) O, you awful, awful, lazy, useless, wretched scoundrel, you refuse to marry me, reject my royal love! O—! (*She breaks down.*)
DRONE	Be advised; Heat not a furnace for your foe so hot That it do singe yourself: we may outrun By violent swiftness, that which we run at And lose by over-running. Know you not, The fire that mounts the liquor till 't run o'er, In seeming to augment it wastes it? Be advised: I say again, there is no beeish soul More stronger to direct you than yourself If with the sap of reason you would quench, Or but allay, the fire of passion.[19]
QUEEN	O that dreadful ... unctuous ... oily ... wretched ... treasonable ... useless ... dirty ... impossible ... bore! (*She rushes about the stage in frenzy.*) I'll kill myself, I'LL KILL MYSELF. (*She screams.*) Do you hear me, I'll kill myself. (*She catches sight of the sleeping* TRAMP *in foreground.*) I'll sting something and kill myself. I'll die, I'll sting this and die! (*She stings the* TRAMP, *who starts up with a cry; then she dies after a brief and noisy paroxysm.*)
TRAMP	What the bloody hell was that? Bees, begob. (*He examines himself gingerly.*) Begob this place is

alive with them divils, I believe wan of them's after stingin' me, pumpin' dirt and poison into me arum. Sure I told yeh — I TOLD YEH there's a bloody nest of them here. Where's me bottle? (*He finds it and takes a suck.*) A little drop on the sting and I was right. But where is the sting? (*He notices the dead* QUEEN *and stands up to peer over at her.*) Holy God, a bee as big as a greyhound. Begob the eyes is goin' — that or me oul' head! What's goin' on in this place at all? (*Enter* BASIL) Holy God, look at your man!

BASIL   (*To* DRONE) Hallao! What have we here? The Queen, by Jove! (*He examines her.*)

TRAMP   I never seen bees that size before.

(BASIL *approaches* DRONE.)

BASIL   The Queen, my lord, is dead.

DRONE   (*Half-asleep*) She should have died hereafter;
There would have been a time for such a word.
To-morrow, and to-morrow, and to-morrow,
Creeps in this petty pace from day to day,
To the last syllable of recorded time;
And all our yesterdays have lighted fools
The way to dusty death. Out, out, brief candle!
Life's but a walking shadow; a poor player
That struts and frets his hour upon the stage,
And then is heard no more: it is a tale
Told by an idiot, full of sound and fury,
Signifying nothing.[20] (*He falls asleep completely.*)

TRAMP   Begob I AM stung. I am stung! I can feel it now. It's here in the middle of me arum; Wan of them dirty bees has got me! (*His voice becomes steely with menace.*) If I could lay me hands on the bee that done that . . . do you know what I'm goin' to tell yeh, if I could lay me two hands on the bee that done that, I'd ——

CURTAIN

38

ACT II

The scene is a sandy hillock with stray stones, holes, patches of coarse grass; to the right and left of the stage are boulders, in between which characters appear or disappear on entering or leaving. Amid the boulders to the left, on somewhat of an eminence, is the nest of The Hen, a dark cave-like dwelling from which bits of straw and sticks protrude; it is not possible to see whether the nest is occupied or not. The TRAMP is lying asleep in the right foreground, unlighted.

As the curtain goes up, there are confused sounds of chirping and clucking from the nest and immediately a large EGG forces itself or is forced to the edge of the nest. It topples over and rolls down on to the stage, where it is seen that a large lump has fallen out of it. It has scarcely come to rest when a beetle rushes in and tries to roll it off; immediately another rushes in to dispute the prize and they quarrel noisily over it with harsh cries. A third beetle rushes in and joins in the fray. In the middle of it, the EGG cries out in a very high shrill voice:

> EGG   I'm being born! I'm being born! Three cheers, hip hip — hurrah! Hurrah! Hurrah!

The beetles scurry back somewhat, curious and a bit frightened: the TRAMP, who has been half asleep, raises his head.

> TRAMP   Pardin? I beg your pardin . . . ?
> EGG   I am being born. The great moment is at hand. The whole world is bursting into blossom!

The beetles have approached the TRAMP after hearing him talk; they regard him curiously from a distance for an instant and then scurry off the stage in alarm.

> TRAMP   Yer been born? (*Then very doubtfully*) I see.
> EGG   I'm in the middle of me crisis. I'm threatened with existence. Light is beginning to breed in me eyes. I'm being born!
> TRAMP   Sure that has to happen to us all, I done the same thing meself single-handed years ago. Years ago man.

He settles down again and there is a pause; from outside is heard the

sound of two beetles talking querulously; they enter – MR *and* MRS
BEETLE, *rolling a huge ball of dirt.*

MR BEETLE   (*In an appalling Dublin accent, apparently even flat-
ter than the* TRAMP's) Here we are now, O.K.,
everything's game ball.

MRS BEETLE   (*In a similar accent*) Do you know, the sweat is
drippin' out of me. Drippin' out of me it is.

MR BEETLE   An' isn't it worth puttin' yourself into a lather
for — a pile of stuff that cost us the grey hairs of
a lifetime to put together? I'm steamin' meself
and I'm only sorry it's not heavier to make me
steam more. (*Rapturously*) Ah begob it's lovely.
It's very . . . very . . . adjacent.

MRS BEETLE   Our gorgeous pile, our lovely savins.

MR BEETLE   The savins of a bloody lifetime.

MRS BEETLE   It's what they do call capital in the bew-uks.[1]

MR BEETLE   (*Turning to address her impressively*) Do you
know what I'm goin to tell you. Do you see that
ball?

MRS BEETLE   (*Abstractedly*) Our gorgeous . . . lovely . . . big . . .
gorgeous pile of savins and capital.

MR BEETLE   Now that pile of stuff there cost me a lifetime of
workin' and slavin' . . . and overtime . . . and
danger-money . . . and time-and-a-half . . . and
Sahurda-work[2] . . . and night-work . . . and
piece-work . . . and all classes of work that isn't
known be anny particular name. Do you know
that?

MRS BEETLE   Sure don't be talkin', there's nothin' like the
capital. It's lovely — I wouldn't be without a
life's savins for all the money in the world.

MR BEETLE   Sure luckit. I seen meself wan June fourteen
shifts on top of one another without a wink of
slape or a bite in me mouth to kill the starvation
— just to get a little bit more on to the pile.
Begob I did and manys the time.

MRS BEETLE   Ah certainly, certainly. An' look how gorgeous
an' big it is now.

MR BEETLE	It grew . . . an' it grew . . . an' it grew.
MRS BEETLE	An' it's ours — ours only. It's our big ball of savins and nobody else owns anny of it.
MR BEETLE	I'm bloody sure it's ours.
MRS BEETLE	Our lovely gorgeous capital.
MR BEETLE	Too bloody true it's ours.
MRS BEETLE	It's gorgeous. Sure is it anny wonder some beetles do be selling their bodies to other beetles that does have a big pile like this?
MR BEETLE	No beetle could make a ball like mine at that game. Sure look at the size of it.
MRS BEETLE	An' it's all ours, our gorgeous savins, the nest egg for our ould age.
MR BEETLE	Smell it, woman, lick it, taste it! It's ours!
EGG	(*Screaming shrilly*) I'm being born! Born, do you hear me! Everything's waking, and quaking, and shaking. I'm expected at every minute, I'm nearly here. Hurray!
MR BEETLE	(*Still preoccupied with ball*) It's very . . . adjacent . . . having a bit of capital, d'ye understand me. It's very . . . ad-mire-able.
MRS BEETLE	I'm as happy as Larry at the present time, there's nothing more to wish for.
MR BEETLE	O steady there now, me gerl, I wouldn't say that. We have wan. Couldn't we have two?
MRS BEETLE	Two! What for?
MR BEETLE	Isn't two better than wan? Or even three. What's wrong with three?
MRS BEETLE	Begob I always knew you had a head on you. Two piles! Three! I never thought of that. TWO big piles, all our very own!
MR BEETLE	Luckit. I'll tell you what. The right game for us is to hide this one and then go off and make another. Do you see?
MRS BEETLE	Hide it? Yes, hide it is right. We'd better hide it right away. Ey, supposin' somebody was to lift it on us . . . ?
MR BEETLE	Lift our little pile? O begob then you won't find me leavin' it lyin' around to be whipped be

41

	some bloody scoundrel. We'll find a hole and bury it.
MRS BEETLE	Yer right, I'd die if annybody lifted our gorgeous pile. Where are we goin' to hide it?
MR BEETLE	We'll invest it, put it away, store it, bury it, d'ye understand, put in into a nice deep hole. You stay here and don't take your eyes off it. I'm off to find a nice hole.
MRS BEETLE	O, I hope it'll be safe, our hard-earned lovely capital. Where are you goin' now?
MR BEETLE	To look for a nice dark hole that nobody else knows about. I'll be back in a tick. Mind the pile now, don't take yer eyes off it. (*Exit*)
MRS BEETLE	Ay, here, come back, don't leave me alone. Ah, begob, the bugger's gone. Sure there's a nice dark hole up there. It looks all right to me. Wait now till I have a decko.[3] Wait till I have a peep now. What we want is a very dark . . . sacred . . . sanitary . . . quiet hole, wan that nobody knows annything about . . .

Her voice trails off as she makes her way up to the nest and disappears into it. Enter a STRANGE BEETLE.

STRANGE BEETLE	(*Jauntily*) O here's me chance, the very thing the doctor ordered. There's nobody here. We take it like this . . . and we roll it away. (*Begins to roll it off.*)
TRAMP	(*Starting up*) Ay, listen here, mind where yer goin!
STRANGE BEETLE	Take yer feet out of me way.
EGG	To be born — to live — to get into the bright blue world! I'm coming, I'm nearly here!
TRAMP	What sort of dirty muck is that yer shovin' around?
STRANGE BEETLE	That's me capital, me pile, everything I have. That's me savins, d'ye understand.
TRAMP	Yer savins? I see. Well there's a bloody awful hum[4] off yer savins then.
STRANGE BEETLE	(*Offended in a very genteel way*) I beg yer pardin?

TRAMP	There's a fierce smell offa that ball.
STRANGE BEETLE	Who ever heard of a smell being off a life's savins. Sure all this stuff is me capital. It's grand stuff, I'm a happy man, it does me heart good to feel it and see it . . .

Exit rolling the ball. MRS BEETLE *emerges from nest, fussing.*

MRS BEETLE	There's somebody livin' there, that wouldn't do at all. AY! Where is it? Where's the pile? WHERE'S THE CAPITAL GONE?
TRAMP	Yer man took it.
MRS BEETLE	(*Rushing at him*) Thief, thief! Where is it, give it to me before I call me husband!
TRAMP	Now fair enough, take it easy. I'm tellin' you where it is. Yer man took it.
MRS BEETLE	Who, who? Where is it?
TRAMP	Yer man that's after walkin' out there, a dark fat round fella with a bit of a belly on him.
MRS BEETLE	Do you mean me husband?
TRAMP	An ugly lookin' customer with crooked feet.
MRS BEETLE	That's me husband all right, he must have found his hole. Where is the bloody fool gone to?
TRAMP	There's the way he went — out there.
MRS BEETLE	Wait till I get him. Why didn't he tell me? Our lovely gorgeous capital, our nest egg. (*Hurries out*)
TRAMP	(*Musing*) Well begob can you beat that! The bloody bees do spend the time blathering out of them but your men the beetles is all for work, gatherin' up all classes of muck and dirt an' rollin' it into big balls, balls that would take the sight out of yer eyes with the smell that's off them. That's the queerest game of the whole lot bar none. And there's a bloody awful stink in the air here after them.
EGG	Let the world prepare, let everything be ready! Be ready, prepare!
TRAMP	Is it you again? What's bitin' you now?

EGG	I'm being born. BORN!
TRAMP	Fair enough.
EGG	I am going to do enormous things — vast, strange, terrible things. I am going to be momentous when I'm born.
TRAMP	I see. Being born, of course, is a very hard thing . . . but it's very interestin'. Ah yes. An' it's a great thing to be born right, of course. Ah certainly.
EGG	I intend to be . . . implacable, wayward, devilish. And powerful, famous, a lord over the world.
TRAMP	I see. Well don't let me stop you. But get yourself born first, you'll never get annywhere without being born. God be with the days when I was born meself.

The DUCK *enters, dragging along a dead ladybird with its claw. It enters the nest.*

DUCK	Look, chick, daddy's bringing you something nice.

The DUCK's *voice is sinister and high-pitched and it speaks with a most refined foreign accent.*

EGG	My birth-pangs are making the earth and the heavens quake. The stars halt in their courses. The fearful hour of my deliverance is at hand.
TRAMP	(*Irritably*) Now that'll be enough out of you, me bucko. There's more oul' chat out of you than I heard from annything the same size.
DUCK	(*Returning*) No, chickabiddy, mustn't come out, just eat what daddy gave you now. Be a good little chick now.

An ugly yellow-headed chick puts its head out of the nest.

DUCKLING	(*Puling*) Daddy, I'm . . . tired.
DUCK	Now, now darling, back to bed. Daddy is going to get you another nice ladybird. Would my little pet like that?

DUCKLING   I don't know what I'd like Daddy. I'd . . . I'd like something nice.

DUCK   Ha-ha! Back to bed now, my little treasure. The dote[5] doesn't know what she'd like. But I really must get something good for her, something interesting, something frightfully delicate. I must hunt. (*To TRAMP*) Who are you?

TRAMP   Who — me?

DUCK   Does one eat a thing like you, I wonder?

TRAMP   (*Sniggering*) Ate me? Not if you have the pledge[6] because you'd only get drunk if you et a man like me.

DUCK sniffs at him.

DUCK   Nao, black shaow, frightfully stale smell. Who *are* you?

TRAMP   Yerra sure I'm only a fella havin' a bit of sleep here on me tod.[7]

DUCK   Ao? Any family?

TRAMP   Not at all man, sure I haven't even a wife.

DUCK   Did you happen to notice the daughter? Fearfully brilliant child, can talk and all that. Deliciously witty person. I do think she is frightfully fetching. Like childen?

TRAMP   Ah well of course the young wans is all right, I wouldn't be heard sayin' a word against them. They're a very nice crowd, some of them.

DUCK   D'you knaow, I do think that children are wizard, full of beans, d'you knaow, and all that. I do think it's frightful fun goin out to get things for them, beetles and all that sort of thing. I mean, parenthood gives one pleasure, you knaow. Give her two or three meals a day.

TRAMP   O'course a growing child'd want that, the bones does be soft and they do have to get lime into them in the feeds. Ah certainly.

DUCK   Matter of fact I'm frightfully proud of her. She'll be a great lady when she grows up — hunting and fishing and skin-foods and that sort of

DUCKLING	thing. But really, I must toddle off and get her something to eat.
DUCKLING	(*From nest*) Daddy, I'm fed up, I'm bored. I want something. I'm tired, daddy.
DUCK	(*Delighted*) Hear that? Pretty average wizard talk for a child if you ask me. Really, old man, I must toddle off and get her something very special. Cheerio, sweetness! Be good till daddy comes back. (*Exit*)
TRAMP	(*Reflectively*) I see. (*He suddenly bellows out in mock rage*) What are you squawkin' out of you about, you bloody little yella bad-tempered bastard?
DUCKLING	(*In a bored supercilious voice*) Shut up, you awful person.
TRAMP	(*Shouting*) I'll shut you up with wan twist of your scraggy neck, you bloody withered peacock, if you don't look out for yourself!
EGG	(*Shouting*) Be ready for me! The great moment of crisis is at hand. PREPARE! BE READY!
TRAMP	You again? Don't *you* start now, because begob I won't have the pair of yez roarin' out of yez at me.
DUCKLING	(*In a low voice to herself*) Perfectly impossible person really.
TRAMP	(*Meditatively*) I don't know . . . I don't know. It's haird . . . it's haird, but it's very interesstin'. It's haird but it's very interesstin'. Your man the bird works the feathers off his back to feed this dirty heap of yellow muck inside in the nest. That's nature for you, of course. And I suppose the people that owns this zoo does be layin' out good hard earned money to feed the hen. And then there's this bastard in the shell lettin' roars out of him every minute. Everybody's well looked after bar meself. It's haird. It's very haird but it's very interesstin'.

Enter MR BEETLE.

| MR BEETLE | (*Calling*) Where are you Maggie? Where the hell |

	are you? Ay, where's me ball? Where's me wife?
TRAMP	Yer wife? Don't tell me that that big fat bags that was here a minute ago is yer wife? You don't mean to stand there and tell me you get into bed with *that*. If you do, keep far away from me, me boy.
MR BEETLE	That's her alright — where is she? Do you hear me? And where's me pile? WHERE'S ME PILE?
TRAMP	She's humped off lookin' for you.
MR BEETLE	But me pile, me ball of capital! Where is it? Do you hear me, where's me bloody capital?
TRAMP	The muck with the bad smell offit? Sure some chancer came along and rolled it off with him. Yer oul wan[8] wasn't here at the time.
MR BEETLE	WHAT! What are you sayin' man?
TRAMP	The stuff is gone and that's all.
MR BEETLE	It's gone? Great God! O great God! Gone! Stolen! Me capital, me savins I'm ruined, I'm destroyed! (*Cries out hysterically*) They've stolen me savins, me capital, they've stolen me investments, me pile! I'm ruined, ruined, where was that bloody bitch of a wife of mine? I'm ruined, ruined. Thief, thief, stop him. Stop him! Murder! Murder! (*Exit moaning*)
TRAMP	I see. As I said before, it's all very haird but it's very interesstin'. It's very interesstin.' Your man kills himself gatherin' up a ball of muck. Then when he has rolled it up nice and big and smelly, along comes your other man and nabs it. And your man, of course, gets nothing for all his trouble and his bloody exertions. It's haird, it's haird.

Enter MR *and* MRS CRICKET. *Both speak with the rawest of all possible Cork accents.*

MR CRICKET	Mind oorself now.
MRS CRICKET	Yerra sure I'm all right.
MR CRICKET	But oo know the way oo are now, sure didn't the doctor tell you to be careful.

47

MRS CRICKET	Well do oo know, I'm worn out with the travellin.'
MR CRICKET	But why wouldn't oo be after comin' all de way from Cork? Sure 'tis a hoor⁹ of a journey. Let you sit down now.
MRS CRICKET	Do oo know, if I'd known this is the way I'd be, not a bit of me would let you do it.
MR CRICKET	Yerra, gwan out of that wid oo.
MRS CRICKET	I'm as tired as a corpse.
MR CRICKET	Oo poor little wife, let oo sit down there now and be aisy. Sure won't it be grand altogether when we have the youngster, chirping and crowin' and laughin' out of him on the floor.
MRS CRICKET	Yerra but won't it be the fine father you'll make, yourself and your youngster.
MR CRICKET	And look at the fine . . . grand . . . impartant job he'll get in the civil service.
MRS CRICKET	Yerra I'm tired — doan't be annoyin' me. Is dis our new home?
MR CRICKET	It is faith. And a grand fine little home it is.
MRS CRICKET	But is it sound, is it dry?
MR CRICKET	As dry as a bone, girl.
MRS CRICKET	I hope it is — oo know I doan't like damp.
MR CRICKET	Yerra doan't be talkin', sure didn't another cricket live here, a cricket from Cork.
MRS CRICKET	(*Moaning*) O, O, the pains is at me — hard. And phwat happened him. The cricket from Cork. Did he get a fine job in the service and move to a bigger house?
MR CRICKET	(*Laughing*) Ha ha! No, he didn't get e'er a jab in de service at all. Do oo know phwat happened him. Could oo guess?
MRS CRICKET	Ah doan't be annoyin' me. Phwat happened him?
MR CRICKET	I'll tell oo. A bird took a fancy to him and et him up. Et him up, every bit and bitteen of him. Ha-ha-ha! And wasn't it lucky for oo and me? (*He makes chewing noise and laughs.*)
MRS CRICKET	Phwat? Et him up . . . alive?

MR CRICKET	Sure twas a shtroke of providence, girl. Only for de bird eatin' him we'd have ne'er a house over our heads at all.
MRS CRICKET	But Lord save us, eaten up alive! Sure that's terrible altogether, dat's a fright. OO! Phwat's dat. Oooooo!
MR CRICKET	(*Alarmed*) What's wrong, girl? What's de matter?
MRS CRICKET	O no, it couldn't be. It couldn't be yet. The pains is at me again — hard. Do oo know, I'm frightened.
MR CRICKET	Doan't worry now, oo'll be allright. Every woman, oo know, has to go through all dat class of ting sooner or later. Sure 'tis only nature, girl.
MRS CRICKET	O, oo can talk, 'tis easy for oo to blather out of oo like dat. Did he chew him or did he swally him in one lump?
MR CRICKET	(*Gloatingly munching*) He chewed him well.
MRS CRICKET	Do oo know, dat's funny. (*Laughs hysterically*)
MR CRICKET	Easy now, girl. We'll be very comfortable here now, when we put up nice curtains and furnishins'. Do oo know what I'd like?
MRS CRICKET	Phwat?
MR CRICKET	I'll tell oo. A nice . . . big . . . juicy kiss.
MRS CRICKET	Yerra go away and doan't be such an ownshuck.
MR CRICKET	(*In an artful whisper*) Do oo know what I have here, inside in me pocket?
MRS CRICKET	I woan't listen to any bold talk and me dis way, you mind phwat you're sayin' now boy.
MR CRICKET	Guess now. Oo woan't? A rattle!

He takes out a rattle.

MRS CRICKET	A rattle! A little rattle! Give it here to me.

MR CRICKET prances round the stage in comic attitudes, humming and making outlandish noises. MRS CRICKET sits and laughs in a somewhat unbalanced fashion.

MRS CRICKET	Wait till de baby comes till he sees de rattle we have. Give it here to me?

MR CRICKET	(*Merrily*) Wait till HE sees it? Sure 'tis a little girl I do be praying for iviry night.
MRS CRICKET	Give it here to me.

He gives it and she starts rattling it and humming in a broken voice.

MR CRICKET	Well do oo know, I must be off now to look around and look up some of de old Cork crowd in de service. They'll tip me off, oo know, about dis place, and bring me around till I get de hang of it. 'Tis impartant to start right away and get in with de right crowd. 'Tis a terrible sin to waste time, oo know.
MRS CRICKET	Phwat, leave me here — alone?
MR CRICKET	Yerra girl sure I'll be only round de corner.
MRS CRICKET	Sure you're no father at all to leave me here and me in a certain condition. 'Tis very unfair entirely.
MR CRICKET	Doan't be mad girl, oo wouldn't like me to miss dem all and dem coming out at five o'clock. Sure dat wouldn't do at all at all. I'll be back nearly before I'm gone.
MRS CRICKET	Well oo must hurry back to mama.
MR CRICKET	And if oo wants me badly oo can rattle.
MRS CRICKET	(*She rattles and hums 'Husha-bye-baby'.*) Oo'r a bad father, that's what oo are.
MR CRICKET	(*Hurrying off*) Mind oorself now, girl, I'll be back very soon with all de news.
TRAMP	Ye'll be game ball there ma'am, ye'll be . . . absolutely . . . O.K. Just stop where you are till yer man comes back and you'll be O.K.
MRS CRICKET	Who are oo? A beetle?
TRAMP	Indeed and begob and I am not a beetle ma'am, I'm certaintly not a bloody beetle and I've been called manny a thing in me time.
MRS CRICKET	Do oo eat people up or bite?
TRAMP	I don't, and I don't spend me time shovin' round balls of dirt either.
MRS CRICKET	(*Rattling*) How many children have oo?
TRAMP	(*In mock indignation*) I beg yer pardin?

MRS CRICKET	Have oo many young wans in de house?
TRAMP	Sure I never had ne'er a kid nor annything like one, I was never a man for that class of thing at all. I always barred that game.
MRS CRICKET	Oo never got married?
TRAMP	*Married*? Not at all.
MRS CRICKET	'Tis very sad not to be married.

She rattles and sings idly as if attaching no importance to the conversation.

TRAMP	(*Very meditatively*) Of course marriage is a very interestin' thing . . . but it's haird, it's very haird. There does be very heavy responsibilities on the married men. They do have to give over takin' a jar[10] when they're married.
MRS CRICKET	You're a very funny beetle. Men are very selfish. Would oo look at my man now, went away and left me and me in a certain condition.
TRAMP	Him? Sure he's only hopped round the corner for a jar to steady his nerves.
EGG	(*Shouting*) The whole future is boiling up inside me! Terrible and vast undertakings are about to be launched forth. The golden hour is about to dawn. I'm coming! I approach!
TRAMP	Do you hear your man?

Enter MRS BEETLE.

MRS BEETLE	Where's me oul fella? Do you hear me? Where's me oul fella? WHERE'S ME PILE?
MRS CRICKET	Oor pile? Phwat pile now?
MRS BEETLE	Me pile, me capital, me own and me husband's life savins, our little all. Where is it? Where's me oul fella?
MRS CRICKET	I'm a stranger here, I didn't see him at all.
MRS BEETLE	The bloody oul eejit must have gone off with it. Have you e'er an oul fella yourself, ma'am?
MRS CRICKET	I have o' course. He's gone away on very impartant business, do oo know.
MRS BEETLE	Is he now. Listen, deary, I know it's none of me

51

	business, I know you'll think I'm very cheeky but tell me, ma'am are ye . . . expectin'?
MRS CRICKET	O! De pains is terrible.
MRS BEETLE	Ah there now, love didn't I know, sure many's the time I was in the same boat meself and I'd be in it this minute if I let his nibs have his way. But not me. I've learnt me lesson.
MRS CRICKET	Well do oo know, tis nice, but tis a terrible price altogether to pay for the grand times you do have when you get married.
MRS BEETLE	Ah the poor girl . . . and you so young. Sure 'tis only a mug's game. Sure look at my figure.
MRS CRICKET	'Tis too late for me to change me mind.
MRS BEETLE	Where's yer pile?
MRS CRICKET	A pile. Phwat do I want a pile for?
MRS BEETLE	What do you want it for? A PILE? Sure everybody has to have a pile. Yer capital, nest egg, for yourself and yer oul man. Yer life savins, something for the rainy day. You don't mean to say yer oul man hasn't a pile?
MRS CRICKET	If he has he never showed it to me.
MRS BEETLE	Sure you can't have a proper home without a pile. Nor you can't have happiness nor a future. A pile is what keeps a home together, woman dear.
MRS CRICKET	Ah yerra sure there's nothing like a grand nice little houseen for keepin' a home together, and a nice job in the service for the man with a grand pinshin¹¹ at the end of it.
MRS BEETLE	Ah musha¹² but you've got the queer ideas, God bless you. I'd no more . . . I'd no more be without a pile than I'd be without me dinner on a Sunda.
MRS CRICKET	Ah there's nothing like the clean bright little houseen to make a man love ye and stay with ye.
MRS BEETLE	Lord love you, I hope you're right, but I want me pile. Where is it? Where's that oul man o'mine? (*Shouts*) Ay, where are you. Ooo-oo! (*Exit*)

| MRS CRICKET | Well, do oo know, isn't that the cantankerous oul sow, I wouldn't blame her husband for skippin off with himself. (*She rattles and sings to herself tunelessly.*) I feel queer. I feel very queer in meself. |

Enter DUCK.

| DUCK | Ao, what have we here? Tally-ho, tally-ho! |

He kills MRS CRICKET and starts to drag her body up to the nest with his leg.

TRAMP	Ay, luckit here, what are you doing? You've killed her!
DUCK	Oh-ho, chickabiddy! Chick chick chick! Wake up darling, daddy's brought something nice.
TRAMP	Well begob can you beat that! He done her in in front of me eyes and me sittin' here lookin' at him. And I didn't move a hand to save her. Begob I'm worse than he is. I'm worse than he is. It's a bloody shame.

Enter PARASITE, who is a frightful-looking sight and the last word in mealy mouthed joxers.[13]

PARASITE	You took the words outa me mouth. Them's me own sentiments sir.
TRAMP	To be whipped off like that and her goin' to have a baby — sure that's not right at all.
PARASITE	It's not right, it never was right, and it never will be right. I understand how you feel. You're a man after me own heart.
TRAMP	And who might you be?
PARASITE	I'm a poor . . . unassumin' . . . labourin' man, I ask no favours and I mind me own business. I'm a poor orphan into the bargain. They do call me a parasite.
TRAMP	I see. Well do you know what I'm goin' to tell you, I never in me born days seen a dirtier stroke than your man done, killin' the young wan off like that.

53

PARASITE   I'm with you there, sir, it aggravated and con-
           sternated me feelins', sir. And answer me this,
           sir. Did he have to do it? Was he starvin' with
           the hunger like meself that hasn't had bite to eat
           or sup to drink for four days? Indeed and begob
           and he wasn't, not bloody likely, he has his
           place inside there packed to the roof with stuff
           smoked and hung up to dry, any God's amount
           of it man. Don't be talkin' to me, sure don't I
           know. And it's a right bloody shame, that's
           what it is. Look at me. I'm half as strong as a
           bantam and twice as light from all me hardships
           and hunger and here is this bastard with more
           stuff than could feed a hundred for a week. Sure
           don't be talkin' to me man.

TRAMP   You're right there — it's a shame certainly.

PARASITE   Luckit. Here am I. I'm poor. I'm starvin'. What
           can I do? Just go on starvin'. But what does your
           man do? He just sticks his claw into the first
           unfortunate poor whore[14] he meets and off with
           him then to have a feed he's not able for. One
           law for me, a different law for his nibs. Sure
           don't be talkin' to me man.

TRAMP   You wouldn't believe all the murder and rob-
           bery and rascality that's goin' on here for the
           last half hour, I'll be as gray as a badger before
           I'm much older.

PARASITE   Sure luckit. You took the words out of me mouth.
           What goes on here day in and day out is a terrible
           crime against the people, mark my words now.
           That bugger[15] above there in that hole'll have to
           be put a stop to, I'm tellin' you. Somebody'll have
           to kill that bugger. Because do you know what
           I'm goin to tell you, he has half the food in the
           country cornered and hoarded and stored away
           there, he has bags and pucks of stuff there inside
           in the nest, lashins of grub goin' bad there while
           meself and me likes is starvin' with the hunger.
           Sure don't be talkin' to me man.

TRAMP	I didn't know he had all that tucked away.
PARASITE	Well, I'm tellin' you he has. To hell with him! To bloody hell with him!

The DUCK re-appears from the nest.

DUCK	That's right, little pet, eat it all up. Good little fluffy chick!
PARASITE	Good evenin', yer honour.
DUCK	Ao, what have we here? Who is this frightful person? Don't move, I'm only smelling you.
PARASITE	Ah now, mister, you're only coddin me. Nobody would ever ate me, mister.
DUCK	D'you knaow, there's a most frightful beastly smell from you. I do think you're pretty average filthy. Be off with you!
PARASITE	Certainly, sir, yer honour, no offence, mister. (*He cowers.*)
DUCK	(*To TRAMP*) I trust you saw my little exploit, old man. Not bad, you know. Frightfully difficult thing sometimes. Calls for skill, you knaow, coolness, iron nerve and all that sort of thing. One has to be in training and so on.
PARASITE	You're right, yer honour, you're right there.
DUCK	Frightful lot of patience called for too, you knaow, fellow has to watch his chance and keep his head and all that sort of thing. I do it rather well, if I do say so myself.
PARASITE	You took the words out of me mouth, your majesty, it's a very haird exacerbatin' occupation.
DUCK	I say, do shut up, you filthy creature. I'm not talking to you.
PARASITE	No offence, yer royal highness. I sincerely beg yer pardin.
DUCK	It calls for qualities one doesn't find in the working classes. I mean, breeding and good form and love of sport and so on. I mean, one is that sort of person or one isn't, you knaow. I do think it is all frightfully fascinating. Well, sir, I think I'll say ·cheerio. Must get a little something more

55

	before dark. No rest for me, you knaow. Pip pip, old boy. *(Exit)*
PARASITE	The dirty mouldy oul bags. For wan minute there I thought I was goin' to let fly at him, I was never so boilin' mad in me life.
TRAMP	O begob he was lucky to escape with his life.
PARASITE	Sure don't be talkin' to me man, another couple of seconds and I'd lost control . Your man was blowin' about all the work he does to get grub. Well, who's afraid of work anyway? I'd work me fingers to the bone meself and welcome if there was anny need to. But why should I when he and his like has a thousand times what I've got? Why should I kill meself to preserve . . . and per-petuate . . . a dirty rich man's world where the poor is ground down . . . and per-secuted . . and starved be the boss class. Do you know what I'm goin' to tell you? I'm a com-munist. I take me stand on communism. And I'm starvin' with the bloody hunger. Sure don't be talkin' to me.
TRAMP	I suppose you wouldn't say no to a nice steak and chips . . . and a few fried onions . . . and plenty of pepper and salt . . . and a bottle of stout?
PARASITE	Ah now man, don't be talkin' to me, don't be talkin' to me. Because I take me stand on com-munism, the boss class is goin' to let me starve to death. Is you and me goin' to stand for that?
TRAMP	Begob I think you're as much entitled to a feed as the next man.

MR CRICKET enters, rattling and chirping merrily.

MR CRICKET	Are oo here? Where are oo, acushla? Where are oo hidin' on me? Guess what I brought oo!
DUCK	*(Suddenly appearing behind him)* AHA!
TRAMP	*(Roaring in alarm)* Hey — mind yerself, MIND YERSELF!
PARASITE	Now listen be a wise man like me and keep yer

56

| | nose out of what doesn't concern you. Don't get mixed up in annybody else's row. You'll get all the trouble you want without lookin' for it. |
| MR CRICKET | Yerra girl where are oo? |

DUCK *suddenly kills him and drags him off.*

| TRAMP | O Lord save us — Lord save us. Did you see that? What are we goin' to do at all —IS THERE NO WAY OF STOPPIN THIS BLOODY SLAUGHTER? |
| PARASITE | What did I tell you? Did you expect any dacency or principles from that baucaugh-shool?[16] Murder, that's *his* dish. Three crickets he's had already and me standin' here with me backbone out through me stomach with the hunger. Would you blame me for being a communist? |

DUCK *quickly re-appears from nest, speaking back to the Duckling.*

| DUCK | No, old girl, can't wait. More work to do, you knaow. Cheery-pip! I'll be back soon. *(Exit.)* |
| PARASITE | I wonder what class of a place has your man above there in that cave. Keep nix there like a dacent man till I have a screw.[17] |

He enters the nest.

TRAMP	Well bad an' all as real people like me is, we're not as bad as that. We don't be killin' and atin' each other, we just work hard and try and make a couple of bob, scrape together a few little savins, a little pile. Blast it, I'm crazy, that's what them bloody beetles does be at. Be God maybe it's all the wan. I don't know. It's haird. It's very haird but it's very interesstin'.
EGG	I feel absolutely ... bulging ... with life and vitality. I'm nearer being born than ever.
TRAMP	You're havin' a great time in there.
PARASITE	*(Falling down out of the nest, bloated, helpless and hiccupping)* Ha-ha-ha! Boys-a-dear! Th'oul bags kept any God's amount of stuff above there for

57

that lousy-lookin' flea-bitten brat he has there,
all classes of — hup — lovely juicy — hup —
grubsteaks, I declare be the powers that I've —
hup — stuffed meself till I can't walk. Hup!

TRAMP   And how about the yella duckling, did she not
bite the nose off you?

PARASITE Her? I swallyed her too, claw, beak and feathers.
I look after Number One. I leave nothin' behind
me, believe you me.

TRAMP   I see. You're a communist all right, there's no
doubt about that. You dirty-lookin' bags.

CURTAIN

ACT III

Back of stage is undisclosed. TRAMP *is again lying in the foreground, musing.*

TRAMP   It's very haird ... but it's very interesstin' — Them little buggers with all the legs on them is queer men. Don't give a damn for one another — every man for himself. You ate me or I'll ate you.

EGG   (*Shouting*) The universe approaches its supreme crisis. Soon it will be liberated, calm, triumphant. I am about to be born.

TRAMP   Now take your man. He thinks he's Number One. Never heard of annybody he likes as well as himself. He thinks he's the whole bloody world. And look at the size of him, stuffed into a bloody egg, a thing I'd ate for me breakfast without lookin' at it. Of course I know what's wrong with all these lads. They've no proper system or way of workin'. They're not organized if you understand me.

EGG   Strange lights are glowing, strange sweet sounds are thickening the air, a frightful and majestic cataclysm is at hand.

TRAMP   Begob I think I've put me finger on it there. That's the difference between meself and me likes and them lads. We have a system, a proper way of workin'. We have what they call a plan. Every man with his own job, all workin' away together for the good of all. What they call the Nation.

EGG   I will soar aloft, traverse vast spaces, accomplish miraculous tasks. I am nearly born!

TRAMP   Begorrah now, I think that's about the size of it. Human beins' is civilized because they do be workin' for one another and workin' together. But these mad whores here do be atin' one another. And that's just the difference between the

59

two. (*He begins feeling himself and the ground about him.*) Ay, what's this? ANTS, be God! Millions of the buggers — I must be sittin' on an ant|hill . . .

Meanwhile the curtain has risen to reveal the Ant Hill, a featureless and uneven situation crowded with ever-moving ants; they carry confused objects that look like tools and each drags along a round white object. In the centre an ant wearing a card marked BLIND sits and counts continuously. The ants speak with a most pronounced Belfast accent.

BLIND ANT	Wun tew three fore, wun tew three fore . . .
TRAMP	Ay, what's this? What's goin' on here? What are you countin' for, Jem?
BLIND ANT	Wun tew three fore . . .
TRAMP	Ay, come here Jem, what's the countin' for? Is this a factory or what?
BLIND ANT	Wun tew three fore . . .
TRAMP	Do you hear me — WHAT'S GOIN' ON? Look at the way all the lads are movin' in step to the blind fella. Begob you'd swear they were all worked be clockwork!
BLIND ANT	Wun tew three fore . . .

CHIEF ENGINEER rushes in.

CHIEF ENGINEER	Come awn now — quacker, d'ye hear me — quacker, wun tew three fore.

They all move quicker.

TRAMP	(*Shouting*) Ay, you, what's goin' on here? What class of work is this? Is this a bloomin' factory?
CHIEF ENGINEER	Hoo orr yew ond what's yoor busness here?
TRAMP	What do you mean 'business'?
CHIEF ENGINEER	Whuch of the awnts do ye wont tay see?
TRAMP	Now listen here to me, I'm a man, d'you understand, A MAN. I'm not an ant and I don't want to have anny conversations with anny ant, I'm not as far-gone as that yet.
CHIEF ENGINEER	Thus us the Prawvince of the Awnts, yoo've no reight to be here at all if yoo're not an awnt.

TRAMP	Is that so. Well it'll take more than you to shift me.

SECOND ENGINEER *runs in.*

2nd ENGINEER	A grawnd new discovery, Ah've discovered something grawnd!
CHIEF ENGINEER	What us it?
2nd ENGINEER	A new way of mackin' them wurk quacker! Don't count wun tew three fore — count blank tew three fore. Are ye lustenin' to me, Bliend Fella?
BLIND ANT	Wun tew three fore . . .
2nd ENGINEER	Naw naw, yew're wrong, blank tew three fore, blank tew three fore.

The ants move more quickly still.

TRAMP	Do you know what I'm goin' to tell you, you're makin' my head go round worse than anny feed of malt ever did. I'm dizzy!
2nd ENGINEER	Ond hoo is thus mon?
TRAMP	I'm a person from other parts.
2nd ENGINEER	Where frum, did ye say?
CHIEF ENGINEER	He's a thing from what ye mieght call the Hewman Awnt Heap, do ye ondherstawnd me.
2nd ENGINEER	Ond where is thon in Go-id's name?
TRAMP	Ah yerra miles away man. It's here too, of course. You'll find my kind of lads *everywhere.*
2nd ENGINEER	Ah thank yoo're a wee fool.
TRAMP	People like me is the lords of creation. That's a quare one for you!
2nd ENGINEER	Ha-ha-ha, the lowerds of creation!
CHIEF ENGINEER	We're the only peepil thot motter.
2nd ENGINEER	We're the bawsses, do ye ondherstawnd.
CHIEF ENGINEER	We're the mawsters.
2nd ENGINEER	Thae mawsters of the Awnt Kingdom.
CHIEF ENGINEER	The biggest of all the Awnt Kingdoms!
2nd ENGINEER	Ond the bee-est.
CHIEF ENGINEER	Ond the strongest, do ye ondherstawnd!
2nd ENGINEER	Ond the most loyal!

CHIEF ENGINEER	The Awnt State will feight ond the Awnt State wull be rieght![1]
TRAMP	I . . . beg . . . your . . . par-din?
2nd ENGINEER	We wurk to keep in step!
CHIEF ENGINEER	Ond to show we're loyal!
2nd ENGINEER	Ond to show we don't care a domn for thon Awnt over in Rome![2]
CHIEF ENGINEER	Ond to show we're hord-headed, do ye ondherstawnd!
TRAMP	(*Incredulously*) I see. I'm sure them's all very good reasons but I don't understand them right. What's all this rushin' around for?
2nd ENGINEER	Thus us a grawnd big foctory, d'ye see, for mackin' things.
CHIEF ENGINEER	For mackin ships ond trains ond nuts ond bolts.
2nd ENGINEER	Ond onny soert of a thang thot's hard, do ye ondherstawnd.
CHIEF ENGINEER	Because we're very hord-headed awnts.
2nd ENGINEER	Ond because we're port of the Empiere.
CHIEF ENGINEER	Ond because we keep in step.
2nd ENGINEER	Ond show avrybody we're loyal, d'ye see.
CHIEF ENGINEER	Ond because we know what's what.
2nd ENGINEER	Ond because thon awnts in the south is jalous of us.
CHIEF ENGINEER	Ond because thon porties hov tacken down the flag of the Good Awnts ond poot up some other flag.
2nd ENGINEER	Ond because they're not loyal, d'ye see.
CHIEF ENGINEER	They all do what thon awnt over in Rome tals them.
2nd ENGINEER	Ond thot's whey they all tok Latin.
CHIEF ENGINEER	A dad longuage.
2nd ENGINEER	Ond they want to mack us tok Latin too.
CHIEF ENGINEER	Ond hov it taught in the schools.[3]
2nd ENGINEER	Ond hov it shoved down the wee awnts nacks.
CHIEF ENGINEER	A dad longuage.
2nd ENGINEER	Ond no good to onyone that hos to eemigrate to gat a luvin.'
CHIEF ENGINEER	Ond they won't hov anybody tokin' the Good

	Awnts' longuage.
2nd ENGINEER	Naw, they want a dad longuage.
CHIEF ENGINEER	Thot's no good anywhere excapt in Rome.
2nd ENGINEER	Ond thot's whey we're wurkin' so hard mackin' hard things.
CHIEF ENGINEER	Tay show we're loyal.
2nd ENGINEER	Ond hord-headed.
CHIEF ENGINEER	Ond ready to fieght for the rieght to keep in stap.
2nd ENGINEER	In stap with the Awnt Empiere.
CHIEF ENGINEER	On which the sun never sats.
2nd ENGINEER	Tha grawndest empiere in the wurld.
CHIEF ENGINEER	Ond the richest empiere.
2nd ENGINEER	Ond the empiere where there's no Latin tokd.
CHIEF ENGINEER	Up his mojesty the king awnt!
2nd ENGINEER	Ond to hal with thon awnt in Rome!
TRAMP	Yerra I don't know what you're talkin' about and yo don't aither. Sure all ants is the same. They're all little round dark fellas. They only think they're different. You're all crazy, gettin' into a sweat about nothin'.
CHIEF ENGINEER	We'll fieght for the rieght to be loyal.
2nd ENGINEER	Ond the rieght to keep in stap.
CHIEF ENGINEER	Ond for the rieght to axport the hard things we're mackin' in this foctory.
2nd ENGINEER	Ond we'll fieght for our holy ralugion.
BLIND ANT	Blank tew three fore, blank tew three fore . . .
2nd ENGINEER	Quacker! We're wastin' time. Quacker, quacker!
CHIEF ENGINEER	The horder we wurk, the safer we are from those bawd awnts in the south.
TRAMP	But sure them other ants you're talkin' about isn't bitin' you at all. Take it aisy now. And don't keep on repeatin' them slogans you have or I'll be believin' them meself next.
CHIEF ENGINEER	We're defandin' our honour!
2nd ENGINEER	Ond the honour of all our dead awnts of glorious and immortal mamory.[4]
CHIEF ENGINEER	(*Roaring at the ants*) QUACKER! QUACKER!!
TRAMP	(*Musing*) I don't know. What would happen if they all sat down and took a rest? Nothing.

BLIND ANT	Blank tew three fore, blank tew three fore . . .
TRAMP	These poor whores has a lot of oul chat off be heart and they keep sayin' it and sayin' it and workin' for it and workin' for it. And what harm but it means nothin' as far as I can see.
2nd ENGINEER	Quacker, Quacker!
TRAMP	I wonder who told them all them yarns.

An ant collapses, dying.

2nd ENGINEER	Whot's thon? Quacker, quacker!
CHIEF ENGINEER	Blank tew three fore. Carry him off, quack! Tack away the body. Blank tew three fore!
2nd ENGINEER	He died because he's loyal, he died for the empiere of the Good Awnts.
CHIEF ENGINEER	(*Shouting*) Luft him up rieght and tack him out quack! Yew're wastin' time, d'ye see. Hurry, quacker!
TRAMP	Well begob you can't say he wasted anny time himself when he was dyin'. He passed out like a lighted match, the poor bastard.
2nd ENGINEER	He died because he was tryin' to keep in stap.
CHIEF ENGINEER	Ond now he's a glorious awnt of immortal memory. Quacker! Blank tew three fore.

Enter a POLITICIAN, *groping, lost in thought.*

POLITICIAN	Get away now ond don't talk to me. I'm thankin'.
2nd ENGINEER	Thon's our wee head Politeecian.
POLITICIAN	Ah've got a grawnd idea for a new slogan. Don't say a word, don't mack any noise. I'm thankin'.
2nd ENGINEER	Do ye mind that now.
POLITICIAN	A grawnd . . . new . . . poleetical . . . slogan, d'ye see.
CHIEF ENGINEER	A slogan that'll mack them work horder ond be more hord-headed!
POLITICIAN	A slogan that'll mack them fieght ond be right ond be loyal ond keep in stap. Stop, now, I nearly have it!
2nd ENGINEER	Be quiet, the Politeecian is thankin'.

CHIEF ENGINEER	On thot's what we're bodly in need of — a grawnd new slogan, d'ye see.
POLITICIAN	A slogan that'll mack them join the Ormy in thousands and mullions ond hundreds of mullions of thousands, tans of thousands of mullions of mullions.
2nd ENGINEER	Ond die in mullions to keep in stap.
CHIEF ENGINEER	Ond to show they're hord-headed ond loyal.
POLITICIAN	Och, it's swirlin' around unside my head, a grawnd new slogan, Ah'll have it in a minit, don't any-body say a wurd now.
2nd ENGINEER	The Politeecian is thankin' hord.
CHIEF ENGINEER	He's a grawnd genius, the Politeecian, Ah don't know where we'd be without him so Ah don't.
2nd ENGINEER	He's the greatest Politeecian in the whole wurld!
CHIEF ENGINEER	He's the most voluable thing we have.
2nd ENGINEER	Shure if we hodn't him we wouldn't have war. Ond then we couldn't be loyal ond hord-headed.
CHIEF ENGINEER	Aye, war. WAR! We'll soon have war. Ond we'll want thon new slogan.
2nd ENGINEER	For to get mullions and mullions into the Ormy.
CHIEF ENGINEER	The Green Awnts in the south will force war on us ond try ond mack us talk Lotin.
2nd ENGINEER	Ond force it down the throats of the wee awnts.
CHIEF ENGINEER	Ond try ond mack them disloyal.
2nd ENGINEER	Ond shame all our dead awnts of glorious ond immortal mamory.
CHIEF ENGINEER	But us awnts'll fieght ond us awnts'll be rieght.
2nd ENGINEER	Aye surely.
CHIEF ENGINEER	(*Shouting suddenly*) Quacker, quacker, quacker! Blank tew three fore! Get intil trainin' because we're goin' to have war!
2nd ENGINEER	War for our homes and our holy relugion!
CHIEF ENGINEER	War against the dirty Green Awnts.
TRAMP	Now don't tell me there's goin' to be more slaughter. Can't yez stop fightin' and atin' one another at all?

CHIEF ENGINEER	It's us or them, d'ye ondherstawnd?
2nd ENGINEER	Thon's a massinger comin'. A massinger!
CHIEF ENGINEER	A Massinger! With news of war!

Enter a MESSENGER.

MESSENGER	Ah beg to report, sir.
CHIEF ENGINEER	Ond what's your massage, say it quack.
MESSENGER	Ah'm from the Ormy G.H.Q., sir.
CHIEF ENGINEER	Well hurry on, what's your massage?
MESSENGER	The Green Awnts was chasin' a sick beetle for to eat it.
CHIEF ENGINEER	Ond it came into our territory?
MESSENGER	Yes sir.
CHIEF ENGINEER	In clear defiance of international law.
MESSENGER	Yes sir. Ond it died in our territory sir.
CHIEF ENGINEER	Ond they want us to give it back to them? Notwithstanding the fact that mullions of our own awnts are starvin for the want of good food?
MESSENGER	Yes sir.
CHIEF ENGINEER	Ond what did they say? What cheeky impartinent massage did they send about it?
MESSENGER	This is it, sir.

Hands over a letter.

CHIEF ENGINEER	What do the bostards say? (*Opens letter and reads*) The Government of the Green Awnts prasants their compliments ond would like the parmussion of the Yellow Awnts to come intil their tarritory for to retrieve the dead beetle rightly belonging to the Green Awnts aforesaid. Signed by Deevil ... Deevil so-ond-so.[5] Well there's not much in thon latter. They'll get no permussion so they'll not. They'll get no permussion for to tack away the beetle. The beetle is our propty by international law.
2nd ENGINEER	(*Coming forward and peering at letter*) But what's thon? There's a P.S. there.
CHIEF ENGINEER	A P.S.? Och so there is. What does it say? P.S. Eff ye don't give permussion we'll come ond get it anyway. Yours sincerely, the Green Awnts.

66

2nd ENGINEER	A threat! An ultimatum!
CHIEF ENGINEER	War! A holy war!
2nd ENGINEER	Our exastince is threatened!
CHIEF ENGINEER	A tarrible war to preserve our weemen and children. Call everybody to arms!
2nd ENGINEER	Mobilise! To orms, to orms!
CHIEF ENGINEER	The foul and patiless enemy is forcing us to defand ourselves. To orms!

There is general excitement and rushing about on the part of the ants. Several begin to appear with crude weapons. A strange and opulent-looking ant enters.

2nd ENGINEER	Who's thon?
CHIEF ENGINEER	Who are you, sor?
STRANGE ANT	(*In refined English accent*) Matter of fact old boy I represent the Emperor of all the free ants and all that. Dropped into see you about fearfully boring imperial matters,[6] imperial contribution and all that.
CHIEF ENGINEER	(*Sullenly*) We've ped all we owe.
2nd ENGINEER	Ond we've kept in step, d'ye ondherstawnd.
STRANGE ANT	Frightfully sorry but you must pay more, cost of living going up and all that.
CHIEF ENGINEER	We've paid every penny we owe and delivered four mullion balls of food.
STRANGE ANT	Not enough old man.
2nd ENGINEER	It's enough ond planty ond damn the more we'll pay, d'ye ondherstawnd.
STRANGE ANT	Magnificent dead beetle in your territory, must have that, you know, have instructions from higher up to annex it and attach it and so on. Food for the people in the Greater Ant Realm, fearfully important thing to keep them fed. Know how you feel and all that but it must be done, you know.
CHIEF ENGINEER	(*Savagely*) You'll tack thon beetle over our dead bodies, so you wull.
2nd ENGINEER	(*Very excited*) We'll die first, do ye hear, we'll die first!

STRANGE ANT	Do you mean war? Black shaow, war, you know. Fearful slaughter and bloodshed and all that. But rather glorious in its own queer way. Die for your country, you know. The supreme sacrifice. Altars and homes and all that.
CHIEF ENGINEER	Eff yew poot wun finger on thon beetle —
2nd ENGINEER	Ye'll be massacreed, d'ye hear.
STRANGE ANT	By Jove I think this is treason! Treason. You are all frightfully Irish here.
2nd ENGINEER	We're loyal but we're goin' to keep thon beetle.
CHIEF ENGINEER	Is this the thanks we get for keepin' in stup?
STRANGE ANT	(*In delighted amazement*) By George it's a rebellion! These elements here are disaffected. Enemies of the Emperor of all the Ants! I say, this is quite a story! Really I must report back!
2nd ENGINEER	Ye can go back to haal where ye came from!
STRANGE ANT	An insurrection!
CHIEF ENGINEER	Eff ye want war it's war ye'll get, d'ye hear.
STRANGE ANT	If you start insurrecting, you knaow, we'll have to put you down with a firm hand. Suspend habeas corpus and all that. Really, I think we are going to have war here! A BLOODY . . . NOBLE . . . AND DISASTROUS WAR FOR HONOUR AND DECENCY.
CHIEF ENGINEER	To orms, to orms! We're being attacked!
STRANGE ANT	(*Going out*) No matter what you give them these damn people aren't satisfied. They're really hopeless, you knaow. Must report all this nonsense. We'll wipe the blighters out and restore order.
2nd ENGINEER	(*Roaring after him*) May ye roast in haal!
CHIEF ENGINEER	To orms! We'll fieght them ond the Green Awnts as well. We'll fieght everybody!

There is great activity; soldier-ants rush all over the place, bugles blow, sirens sound.

TRAMP	Well do you know what I'm goin' to tell you. Do you know what it is. Them buggers is all mad. Down the road we have a dead beetle with his

	dirty bloody guts stickin' out of him and all classes of wasps and bluebottles tryin' to ate him — a dirty useless-lookin' sight. And these lads here wants to die for that. Nothin' will do them but get slaughtered for a dead beetle! I'd die meself, of course, if I'd any reason to. I'd give me life this minute for a pint of porter and often risked me life for less. But a dead beetle! A DEAD BEETLE! Sure that's a terrible reason for dyin'. The whole bloody lot of them is crackers.
EGG	(*Shouting*) Do you hear the mighty trumpets, the vast noises that announce my coming? The firmament resounds, I am nearly here!
TRAMP	YOU'RE nearly here. Begob when you see what's goin' on here you won't stay long then.

Activity among the ants has increased.

CHIEF ENGINEER	(*Eloquently*) Soldiers, friends, countrymen! We have to call the whole lot of ye to the colours. Not one wacked anemy is attackin' us but TWO. The Amperor of the Awnts is attackin' because we won't give up our own beetle, ond them wacked Green Awnts is flyin' at us too, some of them hardened speakers of Lotin!
2nd ENGINEER	We'll have to call the weemen to the colours too. Ond the wee ants as well.
CHIEF ENGINEER	At this great hour I have to proclaim meself Dactator!
2nd ENGINEER	Three cheers for the Dactator!
TRAMP	Good man yourself! Get out now and bate the lard out of them other fellas.
2nd ENGINEER	We'll fight for our altars ond our homes.
CHIEF ENGINEER	We go to war proudly, seeking death or glory for our altars ond our homes ond the right to keep our own beetles, d'ye ondherstawnd. QUICK MARCH! I now assume commond of all our ormies. We fieght because we are attacked. I am with you till the last drop of me blood.
2nd ENGINEER	We'll all have to keep in stap with one another

ond kill all them bostards that's attackin' us. We fieght for the honour of our dead awnts of glorious and immortal memory. Quack march, to vactory or death!

There is marching all about the stage, drums beat and bugles blow. A particularly large drum[7] dominates the others.

CHIEF ENGINEER (*Screaming*) Goodbye, now, soldiers, good luck, good bye, fieght with all your might, never give in, shed the last drop of your blood, I'm here behind you all the time, make the world safe for your weemen and wee awnts, defand your altars ond your homes, navver give in, navver NAVVER give in.

2nd ENGINEER Quack morch, blank two three fore! We'll fieght ond we'll be rieght! The ormy is ready. Show no quarter!

CHIEF ENGINEER Slaughter the annemy's weemen ond wee ones!

2nd ENGINEER Burn all before ye.

CHIEF ENGINEER Ond kill all them bostards that speak Lotin, d'ye understawnd!

Troops keep marching past on their way to the front. A MESSENGER *rushes in.*

2nd ENGINEER Wipe out everybody ye meet, tear the lights out of them Green Awnts. Ond them Red Awnts, do tham all in, roast them all in haal, cut them into wee bits, slaughter the whole domn lot!

CHIEF ENGINEER Onwards, soldiers, to the soop-reme sacrifice, die for your altars ond your commonder-in-chief. Ond for your weemen and wee awnts. Well, what do you wont?

MESSENGER The Red Awnts has pooshed our forces back ond the Green Awnts is behind them pooshin' them the other way. Half of our forces is destroyed.

CHIEF ENGINEER (*Shouting*) Avverything is goin' according to plan. Two more divisions to the front! Quack march! Your country calls! Onwards to death or

70

glory! Show thot you're worthy of your fathers of glorious ond immortal mamory! Quack march, laft, right, laft, right . . .

Fresh regiments march out beating enormous drums. Great bangs are heard in distance.

CHIEF ENGINEER   Call fresh men to the colours! Get ready the reserves.

EGG   Vast detonations shake the earth, thunderous music interferes with the rhythm of the spheres. The universe is in labour! Soon it will bring me forth!

TRAMP   (*Sotto voce*) I see.

CHIEF ENGINEER   The great bottle is on! Second Angineer, wull ye issue a communique.

2nd ENGINEER   (*In a loud toneless voice*) Our preparations are proceeding according to plan. Ten thousand annemy troops are encircled and faced with annihilation. Our gallant forces, fieghting against tremendous odds, have occupied two thousand fortified points. The defeated annemy is being closely pursued. Mopping up operations are in progress. The morale of the troops is excellent.

Enter MESSENGER.

MESSENGER   The first, sacond, third, fourth ond fifth regiments has been completely destroyed.

CHIEF ENGINEER   The bottle is progressing, a grand enormous bottle of annihilation is goin' on, avverything's goin' according to plan. Send up more fresh troops! Eighth, Ninth ond Tanth Regiments, quack morch!

TRAMP   If all this is goin' accordin' to plan, it's a bloody queer plan, that's all I have to say.

2nd ENGINEER   Quack morch! Dath or glory!

CHIEF ENGINEER   Give out another communique!

2nd ENGINEER   The annemy has lost half a million awnts in dead ond missing. The booty has not yet been counted but it is known thot a thousand annemy aircraft was destroyed on the ground. Mopping up operations are in progress.

A MESSENGER *rushes in.*

MESSENGER The Eighth, Ninth ond Tanth Regiments has been wiped out. War has been declared on us by the Purple Awnts from across the sea because we're at war with the Red Awnts. The Green Awnts has captured the Seventh Regiment ond is torturin' them ond makin' them speak Lotin!

CHIEF ENGINEER (*Roaring*) Quack morch, more regiments ond more drums. A great victory is axpacted! We are stronger now than when the war storted. Our production of aircraft ond munitions is staggerin' and mountin' every day. The tempo of our war effort increases. Call up the 50's.[8] Forward gallant soldiers! The home front is behind ye!

2nd ENGINEER We'll fight to the last drop of our blood. We will never capitulate, d'ye undherstawnd!

CHIEF ENGINEER Send out forty thousand bombers right away!

Enter another MESSENGER.

MESSENGER Two more regiments have been wiped out.

CHIEF ENGINEER Call the wee awnts up for military service. Our gallant troops at the front is performin' prodigies of valour. All must share in this glorious task!

Enter stretcher-bearers carrying a wounded ant. Others follow.

TRAMP Ah begob your man is banjaxed. The unfortunate poor whore is bet.

WOUNDED ANT (*Faintly*) Stop this, stop this. We are being cut to ribbons. A drink!

CHIEF ENGINEER Move up another regiment! Give out another communique, Angineer!

2nd ENGINEER Formations of our aircraft have successfully carried out a heavy bombing raid on annemy territory. Harbour installations ond malatory

72

objactives were successfully attacked. Bombs were seen to burst on the target area. Forty-five thousand annemy planes were shot down in air bottles. All our planes returned safely to their bases . . .

MESSENGER Ond the Pink Awnts has declared war on us because we are at war with their friends the Red Awnts. Ond another thing has happened . . .

2nd ENGINEER Ond what's that?

MESSENGER The Green Awnts that talk Lotin is attackin' the Green Awnts that doesn't talk Lotin.

CHIEF ENGINEER *(Loudly)* Our low ond despacable enemies are divided amongst thamsalves, they have all shot their leaders, there is terrible mutiny goin' on, vactory is in sight.

2nd ENGINEER Avverything's goin' accordin' to plan.

Several wounded ants have been carried in on stretchers. They groan hideously.

TRAMP Ah your poor men, they have the insides shot out of them. Do you hear them lettin' roars out of them!

WOUNDED ANT Shoot me! Put me out of me pain!

TRAMP Ah the poor bugger.

CHIEF ENGINEER I see a further massenger approaching. Get ready more reserves! Morch up another new ormy! Call up the wee awnts of 16!

A PHILANTHROPIST ANT with a red cross on him enters.

PHILANTHROPIST Halp the wounded!

TRAMP Ah yes, the poor wounded buggers.

PHILANTHROPIST Halp the heroes, the glorious ond immortal heroes.

CHIEF ENGINEER Reinforcements! Hurry with the reserves! Here's the massenger.

TRAMP *(Tears off a button from his coat)* Ah yes, the poor wounded buggers. Here y'are, me son!

He puts the button in the box. Enter MESSENGER.

MESSENGER	The Tanth, Eleventh, Twalfth, Thirteenth, Fourteenth, Fifteenth ond Saxteenth Ormies has been wiped out.
CHIEF ENGINEER	Our heroic men continue to fight gallantly. The annemy has sustained enormous losses. Give out another communique!
MESSENGER	Ond the Savventeenth Ormy is now in the middle of bein' wiped out too.
2nd ENGINEER	Last night our troops fought the annemy along the whole front. Several fortified places ond inhabited localities was taken. Our troops are pursuing the defeated annemy. Mopping up operations are in progress.
CHIEF ENGINEER	Get me a wee spy-glass.
2nd ENGINEER	(*Shouting*) A wee spy-glass for the Commonder-in-Chief!
TRAMP	Begob it's a good spy-glass you'll want if it's yerself winnin' you want to see.

A soldier-ant brings a telescope.

CHIEF ENGINEER	The annemy is in headlong retreat!
2nd ENGINEER	Vactory, vactory!
CHIEF ENGINEER	We have captured ond invested five blades of grass.
2nd ENGINEER	Vactory!
CHIEF ENGINEER	The annemy has sustained enormous ond bloody losses. I see nothing but dead Green Awnts ond dead Red Awnts ond dead Pink Awnts. Ond dead Mauve Awnts. Ond dead Brown Awnts. Everybody is dead excapt our own awnts.
2nd ENGINEER	A grond vactory for democracy and decency!
CHIEF ENGINEER	Now they've captured four more blades of gross! Vactory is assured!
2nd ENGINEER	Tell them to take no prusoners. Slaughter avverybody! Slaughter the annemy's weemen ond wee awnts! A holy vactory!
CHIEF ENGINEER	The ramnents of the beaten annemy is bein' pursued. The Red Awnts ond their allies are

	annihilated. There's nothing left to be done.
2nd ENGINEER	— Only moppin' up.
CHIEF ENGINEER	We have fulfilled the glorious and immortal dastiny of our race! Here, take the wee spyglass!
2nd ENGINEER	Isn't it grond to be alive at this glorious ond immortal hour. Our gallant troops have covered thamsalves with glory.
CHIEF ENGINEER	(*Roaring*) Vactory is ours, right ond justice ond fairplay and democracy has prevailed. (*Falls on his knees*) Great God of the Awnts, thou hast deigned to bless the orms of thy faithful sarvants, thou hast given us victory! I appoint thee an honorary member of our gallant ormy, with the rank of colonel. (*He jumps up*) Twenty-first ond Twenty-sacond Ormies, forward! Quack morch, onward to the front! Take your place by the side of your gallant ond victorious comrades! Call up all resarves! Form the weemen ond wee awnts into battalions! All must fight at this glorious ond immortal hour. (*Down on his knees again*) Righteous ond all-powerful God of all the Awnts, thou knowest how well we desarve the vactory thou has deigned to give us! (*Jumps up*) Attack! Take no prisoners! Forward avverybody to the front! Set all the annemy prisoners on fire ond roast them! Tear up the wee prisoner awnts into wee bits! (*Kneels*) Glorious ond immortal God of the Awnts, by our vactory thou hast conferred the priceless boon of peace on the world! (*Jumps up*). Quack morch! Attack! We will navver retreat, we will navver give in, we'll fight to the last drop of our blood for our hearths and our homes. We have won a glorious peace! The world is now a fit place for hero-awnts to live in![9]
TRAMP	(*Bending over* CHIEF ENGINEER *and talking to him softly*) The world? Did I hear you sayin' THE

	WORLD? Sure Lord save us man this isn't the world! Sure this here is only a lump of muck. I could kick the whole bloody issue from here to Carlow with wan root of me boot and you along with it!
CHIEF ENGINEER	Who are you? Why aren't you doin' your duty at this glorious hour?
TRAMP	Who am I? O indeed faith you needn't bother your barney about me. I'm only . . . an oul' chap . . . lyin' here . . . havin' an odd jar to meself here. And I fought hard enough in me own day, too. God be with the oul' Munsters[10] and every dacent man that was in them. Ah, the oul' crowd, you can't beat them. But YOU! What's all this cavortin' and rampagin' about? How many of these poor little bastards have you slaughtered? How many of them have you killed to make yerself a big fella?
CHIEF ENGINEER	(*Haughtily*) I'll pay no attention to the like of you. On behalf of all the Yalla Awnts I now crown meself Emperor.
2nd ENGINEER	(*Looking thorough glass*) Long live the Amperor!
CHIEF ENGINEER	What can you see through the wee glass? Are we havin' any more glorious vactories.
2nd ENGINEER	The vactory is a wee bit delayed. The last ormies we sent out is callin' for reinforcements.
CHIEF ENGINEER	Make them hold out! Tell the generals to shoot down cowards that won't fight! Send the weemen to the front!
AN OFFICER	(*Off-stage*) Quack morch, quack morch!
CHIEF ENGINEER	Ond the crapples ond wee awnts!
2nd ENGINEER	Holy Gawd, all our glorious ormies is in full flight. The Red Imperial Awnts is after them ond after them again is the Green Awnts.
CHIEF ENGINEER	To orms, to orms! Avverybody must fight! Protact the Amperor.

The confused noses of battle are heard coming closer and closer. The screams of wounded fill the air.

76

2nd ENGINEER	Our ormies are bein' massacreed!
CHIEF ENGINEER	Protact the Amperor! The Amperor!
A SHOUT	Back, Back! Stop! Stop!
ANOTHER SHOUT	Run, RUN! Avvery man for himsalf! Run, RUN!
CHIEF ENGINEER	(*Screaming*) Where is the Amperor's personal bodyguard? Fight, ye bostards, FIGHT!

Two yellow soldier-ants rush in. Din of battle increases off-stage.

SOLDIERS	We're bein' slaughtered! Escape!
2nd ENGINEER	Go back ond fight, ye dirty cowards. Fight for your country ond your Amperor! FIGHT!
CHIEF ENGINEER	(*To soldiers*) I commond ye as your Amperor to protact me ond be my bodyguard!
SOLDIERS	Away out o' that, ye wee bostard!

They kill him as they rush out again right.

2nd ENGINEER	Holy God, we're captured! The lights, put out the lights! It's the only chance to escape. The lights!

Several Red ants rush in. The lights go out. There is terrific turmoil and noise.

2nd ENGINEER	Fight on to the last! AH———

He groans, evidently mortally hit. A faint light in the centre of the stage indicates that it is filled with victorious Red and Allied Ants. There is great clanking of weapons and confused noise. Then a refined English voice says:

ENGLISH VOICE	Phew, jolly hard going. We've wiped out the bastards. Deserve what they get, too, dim shaow attacking us, you knaow.
COCKNEY VOICE	(*In alarm*) Gorblimey, the Green Awnts!

There is a rush and some Green Ants are discerned fighting madly with the Red Ants, though most of the fighting is off-stage, judging by the row. When the battle has subsided, the centre of the stage is occupied by victorious Green Ants. A voice with a thick southern brogue is heard.

SOUTHERN VOICE	Do you know, we've slattered and destroyed the whole empire of them, yellow and red and

	blue and every colour. We own the whole world now and every thing in it, it takes us boy.
VOICE	(*In alarm*) Gob phwat do I see? Phwat do I see. Green Ants with fáinnes[11] on them is goin' for our lads out there. They're roarin' out orders in a foreign language.
SOUTHERN VOICE	Come on, lads, fight for ye'r lives!

Another vast battle is fought, mostly off-stage, but in the circle of light Green Ants reel in death-grips with other Green Ants who wear enormous gold fáinnes. Words and shouts that sound like Irish are heard above the din. When the battle subsides, the fáinne-wearers have won. The commanders gather in the circle of light. A RICH VOICE is heard.

RICH VOICE	A dhaoine uaisle agus a chairde Gaedheal! A chairde agus a dhaoine go léir! Tá buaidhte fá dheireadh ag na Gaedhil. Tar éis an chogaidh seo tá an domhan go léir buaidhte aca.[12]
TRAMP	Whaa? I beg yer pardin?
RICH VOICE	Ar an ocáid stairiúil seo fógraighim mise féin im Impire ar an domhan go h-uile![13]
TRAMP	What's yer man sayin' or tryin' to say?
PETULANT VOICE	Do you not know your own language, you ignorant man? He is proclaiming our great victory. At this hour he becomes emperor of all the earth. History is at an end. Our glorious destiny is achieved after seventeen hundred years.
TRAMP	He's EMPEROR?? Of the EARTH . . . I see.
EGG	I'm . . . nearly born.
RICH VOICE	Ní bheidh acht an Ghaeilge amháin á labhairt ar fúd an domhain feasta.[14]

TRAMP has sprung up, kicked the Emperor over and grinds him to bits as the others scurry off.

TRAMP	You . . . dirty . . . bloody . . . lousy . . . little bastard of an insect. Ouwathat!

CURTAIN

EPILOGUE

Darkness everywhere. The TRAMP, *picked out by a faint light, is lying in the foreground sleeping. He stirs uneasily and speaks in his sleep.*

TRAMP Take yer hands offa me now — take yer hands off me: What? What'd you say? I beg your pardin? STOP BATIN' THAT FELLA! Stop killin' him! Gou-athat! Take yer sting and pump it into some-wan else! Keep yer distance or I'll destroy yeh! D'yeh hear me?

Pause.

Then in a pathetic voice:

I don't feel too well at all. I'm not in me right health. I wouldn't like to pass out here in the dairk ... all be meself. Give us a bit of light there, some wan ...

CYRIL (*Far off*) Cec-eel, where are you?

CHIEF ENGINEER Avvery mon, wooman ond wee wan to the front now. Quack morch!

MR BEETLE Ay, where's me pile gone to? D'yeh hear me? Where's me pile? WHERE'S ME PILE?

CYRIL (*Calling softly*) O Cec-eeeeeeel ...

TRAMP Will yez stop blatherin' in the dark and show a light till I see am I alive at all! I don't want to be stung again be that bloody big bee I seen sitting in a deck chair!

DRONE Princes and noble lords, what answer shall I make to this base man? I say, thou liest, and will maintain what thou hast said is false in thy heart-blood, though being all too base to stain the temper of my knightly sword.[1]

TRAMP (*Awed*) I beg yer pardin?

DUCK (*Appearing under a ghostly spotlight in the background stalking an invisible cricket.*) Nearly got the blighter. Four today and one more makes five.

Lunges forward and there is a scream as the light goes out.

TRAMP   You've killed him! (*Excitedly*) You've killed an-
         other one! Can yeh not stop killin' and
         slaughterin'? CAN YEH NOT BE AISY AND
         LAVE OTHER PEOPLE ALONE?

EGG   (*Revealed by dim spotlight and seen to be moving
         slightly*) I'll get out of this if it's the last thing I
         do, if it's the last thing I do I'll break this bloody
         shell. I'll be here soon, make no mistake at all
         about that!

CYRIL   (*Afar off, perplexed*) Do tell me, Cec-eel, where *are*
         you, old boy.

TRAMP   Begob I believe I'm goin' off me rocker.

MR BEETLE Listen here, WHERE'S THAT BALL? Where's
         me capital?

TRAMP   That's that bloody beetle, I'd know the voice
         anywhere.

*The spotlight reveals dimly a beetle sneaking in and starting to roll away
the* EGG.

EGG   Help! HELP! Stop! Stop that!

BEETLE   Shut up or I'll ate yeh here!

EGG   HELP! HELP! I want to be born! He's going to
         kill me! HELP !

TRAMP   (*Rising on elbow*) Ay! You leave that bloody poor
         little egg alone — d'yeh hear me?

*The 'hideous cries' are gathering in the background and now rise in
crescendo. Confusion grows.*

TRAMP   Leave that egg alone. My God, more slaughter,
         more bloody slaughter!

CHIEF ENGINEER (*Invisible*) The agg is port of our nawshional
         haritage! Defand it with your lives! Quack
         morch! Quack morch!

*The dim light reveals that several beetles have rushed to contest the
ownership of the* EGG. *Several ants join in and a great battle starts:
screams and roars and general din.*

TRAMP   (*Rising excitedly*) DIDN'T YOU HEAR ME?
         Didn't you hear me tellin' yeh to lave that egg

alone? OUT OF ME WAY! If yez harum that egg
I'll have yer bloody lives! OUT OF ME WAY!

*He is seen in the gloom to plunge madly into the battle, tripping and
falling down among the milling insects. Soon his own horrible cries
mingle with those of the others.*

TRAMP   Stop that! STOP! Yez are killin' me. YEZ ARE
ATIN' ME! Ow — !

*The row dies down gradually and darkness has descended. There is
silence. Birds twitter and the dawn breaks. The* TRAMP *is revealed in a
crumpled heap with frost on his clothes. Beside the body is an ordinary
broken egg-shell. Two mooning lovers stroll in, the* BOY'*s arm round the*
GIRL'*s waist. They start slightly at the spectacle of the* TRAMP.

GIRL   O George, look!

BOY   Janey, a beggar! He's asleep!

GIRL   Look at the bottle. He's drunk. He must have
been lying there all night. O George, I hate
drunkards.

BOY   How do you know I'm not one myself! Or that I
won't be when we're married. How would you
like me to go out every Friday and drink the
week's wages. And leave nothing to buy food
for you and the kids.

GIRL   (*Coy whimsy stuff*) O George, how do you know
we are going to have kids. You're a very bold
boy.

They begin to move off and exit.

BOY   Well now you know. We're going to have four
kids — two girls and two boys. Not girls and
boys following each other, of course, A boy,
then a girl, and so on.

GIRL   O George . . .

Exit. A ball runs across the stage followed by two ragged small BOYS,
shouting. They stop and regard the TRAMP.

1st SMALL BOY   Aw look at the man.

2nd SMALL BOY   He's asleep

1st SMALL BOY	Maybe he's dead. (*He runs to retrieve ball*.)
2nd SMALL BOY	My daddy's dead and mammy's goin' to marry Mr Conlan.
1st SMALL BOY	I wouldn't mind your ould wan.

They chase the ball off the stage again. Enter KEEPER.

KEEPER	Ay what's this. What's going on here. My God, has this bloody fellow been here all night!

Very concerned, he kneels and examines the TRAMP. *He rises, enormously excited.*

KEEPER	My God, he's dead. There'll be a bloody row about this. (*He picks up bottle and smells it*.) Whiskey. There'll be hell to pay. (*He roars for a brother keeper*.) Hey! Slattery! SLATTERY! Come over here! Quick!

SLATTERY, *a youth, comes running in.*

SLATTERY	What's up?
KEEPER	This unfortunate man's dead. Give me your coat.

He covers corpse with overcoat.

SLATTERY	Dead? Was he here all night?
KEEPER	He was and whoever locked him in is going to get into a row. And it wasn't me, Slattery.
SLATTERY	The poor unfortunate divil.

The lovers come back, attracted by the row; they are soon followed by the small BOYS, *possibly reinforced in numbers.*

KEEPER	Phone for the ambulance, Slattery. STAND BACK NOW PLEASE. EVERYTHING'S ALL RIGHT.
GIRL	Is he *dead*?
KEEPER	Everything's all right now. Stand back please.
GIRL	O George!
BOY	He's better out of it the poor divil.
1st SMALL BOY	The man's dead.
GIRL	O George, the poor man. The poor man.

82

BOY	Do you see the eggshell. I suppose a little chicken was born out of it. Chicken starts out as this man finishes up . . .
KEEPER	It's a Duck's egg. Now yez'll all have to move on please. We don't want any crowds collectin'.
2nd SMALL BOY	Aw come on, come on home. I want to get me boat. Come on Paddy.
1st SMALL BOY	All right come on.

They trail off to exit. Immediately a LITTLE GIRL's voice is heard off, from the other side.

LITTLE GIRL	Paddy! PAD—EE! Wait for me!

She hurries in to follow them and crosses stage, pushing an enormous pram.

KEEPER	Gob, I never seen so many children.

CURTAIN

NOTES

PROLOGUE

1 twopenny type: chairs rentable for twopence.
2 no home to go to: a phrase much used at closing time by Dublin barmen.
3 Guard: a policeman, in Irish *Garda Síochána*.
4 de Valera . . . Bangalore: Eamon de Valera (1882-1975), President of the Executive Council (Prime Minister) from March 1932 until February 1948, and also June 1951-June 1954 and March 1957-June 1959; after December 1937 his title was Taoiseach. The Kildare Street Club, now extinct, was Dublin's most exclusive men's club. The Keeper presumably refers to the Bishop of Bangalore for alliterative reasons.
5 Boord of Works: a government department charged with maintaining parks, public buildings, and other public properties.
6 the 'joy: Mountjoy Prison near the Royal Canal in Phibsboro, North Dublin.
7 Mister Connolly: Joseph Connolly, then Chairman of the Board of Works. In September 1939 he was appointed Controller of Censorship. R.M. Smyllie, Myles's editor at *The Irish Times*, described Connolly as 'a bitter Anglophobe.' See Bernard Share, *The Emergency; Neutral Ireland, 1939-1945* (Dublin: Gill and Macmillan, 1978), 32. Smyllie claimed that 'in practice . . . the censorship . . . worked almost exclusively against the Allies,' and called it 'ludicrous ' He was not allowed to mention that many Irishmen had joined the British forces nor could obituaries speak of death in battle. The Irish births of Generals Montgomery and Alexander 'had to be kept dark'. When a Dubliner serving in the British Navy was rescued from his sinking ship, this could only be mentioned by stating 'in the Social and Personal column that the young man . . . had completely recovered from the effect of his recent boating accident!' See R.M. Smyllie, 'Unneutral Eire,' *Foreign Affairs* 24: 2 (January 1946), 322-3. Myles's 'Cruiskeen Lawn' column was apparently censored (Cronin, *No Laughing Matter*, 119).
8 omadaun: Irish *amadán*, fool, simpleton, idiot.
9 own-shucks: *óinseach* is the female form of *amadán*.
10 drop o'malt: malt is whiskey.
11 family allowances . . . undher th'plough: The Fine Gael leader, James Dillon, suggested government subsidies to assist poor families in March 1939. Myles, in his Civil Service capacity as Brian O Nualláin, was appointed Secretary to the Local Government Committee set up in July 1939 to study the question. The Committee first met in April 1940, and eventually recommended the appointment of a second, interdepartmental committee. The second Committee was even more desultory, reporting finally in October 1942, and recommending the establishment of Family or Children's Allowances. The proposal was strongly opposed, on both political and religious grounds, by J.J. McElligott, Secretary to the Department of Finance, and by Sean MacEntee, Minister of Local Government (August 1941-

February 1948), Myles's/O Nualláin's direct superior. MacEntee's hostile memoranda, presumably drafted by Myles, then his private secretary, were particularly numerous, lengthy, and hysterical in February–March 1943. McElligott's and MacEntee's conviction that rural poverty was morally bracing, and quintessentially Irish, echoes — presumably unconsciously — similar ideas which Myles had parodied in *An Béal Bocht* (1941). Their insistence that the child allowance would weaken the family and so subvert Catholic values anticipated arguments used successfully against the 'Mother and Child' plan of Dr Noel Browne (Minister of Health, February 1948-11 April 1951), which proposed free pre- and post-natal care for mothers and children, irrespective of means. See J.J. Lee, *Ireland 1912-1985* (Cambridge: Cambridge University Press, 1989), 277-86.

The slogan 'One more cow, and one more sow, and one more acre under the plow,' was coined by Patrick J. Hogan (1891-1936), Minister of Agriculture 1922-32.

ACT I

1 This castle . . . senses: *Macbeth* 1.6. 1-3, spoken by Duncan as he enters Macbeth's castle.

2 What early tongue . . . distemperature: *Romeo and Juliet* 2.3.32-40. Friar Lawrence rebukes Romeo for visiting him so early.

3 eight hundred thousand feet: some species of bees do have queens who mate on a nuptial flight, but considerably closer to the ground. I am grateful to my colleague, Prof. Stephen Welter, for assistance with Myles's erratic entomology.

4 little tickets: presumably coupons for the Irish Sweepstakes.

5 'O Death, where is thy sting': 1 Corinthians 15.55.

6 Foul whisperings . . . their secrets: *Macbeth* 5.1. 79-80. The Doctor, after observing Lady Macbeth's sleep-walking scene.

7 This is the state . . . he falls: *King Henry VIII* 3.2. 352-8. Commencing 'This is the state of man,' the speech is Wolsey's meditation on his downfall.

8 If I am . . . go through: *Henry VIII* 1.2. 71-6. Wolsey again, defending the taxes he has levied, when Queen Katherine tells the King they have angered the people.

9 Things done well . . . not any: *Henry VIII* 1.2. 88-92. King Henry rebuking Wolsey and ordering him to lower the tax.

10 What should this mean? . . . see them more: *Henry VIII* 3.2. 204-09; 223-8. Wolsey, as he begins to realize that the King knows of his secret dealings and the fortune he has amassed. Myles substitutes *They* for *He* (205) and *bee* for *man* (226).

11 Meriel Moore . . . 'Jack-in-the-Box': *Jack-in-the-Box*, the Gate Theatre's 1942 Christmas entertainment, included Myles's *Thirst* and Oscar Wilde's 'fragment,' *La Sainte courtisane, or, The Woman Covered with Jewels* (written in 1894-5), in which Meriel Moore played the gaudily seductive Myrrhina.

12 Who's there . . . meditations: *Henry VIII* 2.2. 64-5. King Henry, angry at being interrupted while brooding over his plans to divorce Queen Katherine.

13 I prithee, go to: Shakespearean phrases, but from no specific play. Please, leave me alone.

14 In peace there's nothing . . . full height!: *Henry V* 3.1. 3-17. King Henry urging his men on at Harfleur; the speech begins with the famous, 'Once more unto the breach, dear friends . . . '

15 Let us seek . . . empty : *Macbeth* 4.3. 1-2. Malcolm to Macduff, in their English exile. Uncharacteristically, the Drone has misquoted slightly: 'seek out some desolate shade.'

16 Like the Pontick sea . . . swallow them up: *Othello* 3.3. 453-460. Othello, reacting to Iago's insinuations about Desdemona and Cassio.

17 This argues fruitfulness . . . exercise devout: *Othello* 3.4. 38-41. Othello to Desdemona, suspicious because her palm is sweaty.

18 Stay, my pet . . . tires him: *Henry VIII* 1.1. 129-34. Norfolk, who begins, 'Stay, my lord,' urging Buckingham to behave prudently.

19 Be advised . . . fire of passion: *Henry VIII* 1.1. 139-49. Norfolk, continuing his good advice.

20 The Queen, my lord, is dead . . . Signifying nothing: *Macbeth* 5.5. 16-28. Myles neatly appropriates Seyton's announcement of Lady Macbeth's death, and Macbeth's ensuing meditation.

ACT II

1 bew-uks: books

2 Sahurda-work: Saturday work, overtime.

3 have a decko: have a look, possibly from Romany *dik*, to look.

4 hum: smell.

5 dote: pet.

6 the pledge: Father [Theobald] Mathew's pledge, to abstain from alcohol, which he developed in 1838 to promote abstinence in Ireland.

7 on me tod: on my own, alone.

8 oul wan: spouse, literally 'old one'.

9 hoor: an Irish pronunciation of *whore*, here simply suggesting a difficult journey.

10 takin' a jar: drinking.

11 service . . . pinshin: the Civil Service, and its pension.

12 musha: exclamation, from the Irish *más ea*, even so, or *maiseadh*, if it be so.

13 joxers: yes-men, insincere flatterers (Dublin slang).

14 poor whore: see *hoor*. In this case, not a lady of the evening but someone easily victimized.

15 bugger: literally a sodomite, but here simply a disagreeable person. Replaced in performance by *bowsy*, a Dublin term for an aggressive bully.

16 baucaugh-shool: a wandering beggar, a tramp, from *bacach*, beggar, and *siúil*, to walk.

17 Keep nix . . . a screw: keep watch . . . till I have a look.

ACT III

1 The Awnt State will feight ... be reight!: In an effort to bring down Gladstone's Liberal government, Lord Randolph Churchill (1849-95) decided to 'play the Orange card', that is, appeal to the widespread fear and hatred of Catholics among the Presbyterians of Northern Ireland, especially those who were members of the Orange Order, founded to resist Catholic claims. They were bitterly opposed to Gladstone's plan to give Ireland 'Home Rule', which they believed would put them at the mercy of the Catholic majority. Churchill first used the slogan, 'Ulster will fight, and Ulster will be right', when he landed at Larne (22 February 1886) to arouse the Presbyterians and encourage them to resist Home Rule by every means, even civil war. The phrase became popular, and was revived by Sir Edward Carson (1854-1935) against the Third Home Rule Bill (1912-14), as well as by later opponents of any merging of Northern Ireland with the Irish Republic. Those opposed to such a merging are called Unionists or Loyalists (loyal to the union of Great Britain and Northern Ireland).

2 Awnt over in Rome: the Pope.

3 Latin ... taught in the schools: a conflation of the Catholic Church's liturgical use of Latin at that time, and efforts to revive the Irish language by making it a compulsory subject in the schools of Eire.

4 glorious ond immortal mamory: a phrase from the 'Orange' toast 'To the glorious, pious, and immortal memory of the great and good King William [William of Orange], who saved us from Popery, brass money, and wooden shoes.'

5 Deevil so-and-so: Eamon de Valera. Myles has reversed and so disguised certain contemporary issues, perhaps to evade — or tease — the censors. In 1943, neutral Ireland (Eire) feared invasion by either German or British forces, with the latter much more likely. The British resented the presence of German and Italian diplomats in Dublin, and wanted to use the 'Treaty Ports' (Cobh, Berehaven, and Lough Swilly), former British naval bases on Irish territory, turned over to the Irish in 1938. Northern Ireland, as part of the United Kingdom, participated in hostilities against Germany.

6 imperial matters: the STRANGE ANT represents various British emissaries who tried to persuade or threaten de Valera into assisting the British war effort, since Ireland was still technically part of the British Empire/Commonwealth; here, ironically, Northern Ireland is being treated as insufficiently committed to the War.

7 large drum: a lambeg drum, usually a feature of Orange marches.

8 the 50's: men fifty or older.

9 a fit place ... to live in: 'What is our task?' David Lloyd George (1863-1945; British Prime Minister 1916-22) asked in a speech at Wolverhampton (24 November 1918), and answered himself: 'To make Britain a fit country for heroes to live in.'

10 the oul' Munsters: the Royal Munster Fusiliers, a British Army regiment traditionally recruited from the Province of Munster. Disbanded along with the other 'southern' Irish regiments in June 1922.

11 fáinnes: gold circles worn as lapel pins by Irish speakers.

12 A dhaoine ... buaidhte aca: Noble people and Irish friends! Friends and all people! The Irish have won at last. After this war they have

conquered the whole world.
I wish to thank my colleague, Dr Joan Trodden Keefe, for assistance with Myles's Irish.

13· Ar an ocáid . . . domhan go h-uile!: On this historic occasion I declare myself Emperor of the whole world!

14 Níl bheidh . . . feasta: From now on, only Irish will be spoken throughout the world.

EPILOGUE

1 *Richard II*, 4:1: 19-20, 26-9. The speaker is Aumerle, the 'base man' Bagot. Perhaps weary by this time, the Drone makes prose out of Shakespeare's blank verse:

> Princes and noble lords.
> What answer shall I make to this base man?
> . . .
>
> I say thou liest,
> And will maintain what thou hast said is false
> In thy heart-blood, though being all too base
> To stain the temper of my knightly sword.

From the Dung Heap of History

Peter Lennon (28 February 1930—18 March 2011)
on a newly discovered text from the Irish writer with
a contemporary resonance.
The Guardian, 17 November 1994

A play by Ireland's most celebrated comic writer, Flann O'Brien, lost for fifty years, has been discovered in the archives of Northwestern University, Illinois, by an American academic. It will be published next week by the Dublin Lilliput Press.

It was known that Flann O'Brien, author of *The Dalkey Archive* published in 1965 and *The Third Policeman* (1967), had written a play which was a free adaptation of Karel and Josef Capek's 1921 *The Insect Play*.

This was inspired by a French entomologist's *La vie des insectes*. Its target was Henry Ford's world of the assembly line and time and motion studies.

The O'Brien play, *Rhapsody in Stephen's Green*, was put on in Dublin by the Edwards-MacLiammoir company at the Gaiety Theatre during Lent in 1943 with a cast of 150 — representing millions, as is obligatory with an insect play. But, presumably because of the offence it gave to Catholics, Ulster Protestants, Irish civil servants, Corkmen, and the aspersions it seemed to cast on married life and the superpatriotic Fianna Fáil party, it only ran six days and was never again performed. O'Brien died in 1966.

Robert Tracy, Professor of English and Celtic Studies at the University of California in Berkeley, told from his California home how he discovered the play: 'I was actually researching performances of Chekov in Ireland,' he said. 'I wanted to get records of the Edwards-MacLiammoir productions, but I was told all the company's papers had been sold to Northwestern University. Going through the index of contents I saw the insect play mentioned.

'I at first assumed this was just the first act, well known by scholars, but you can imagine the thrill when I found they had a full text which was clearly Hilton Edwards' prompt copy.'

89

The first act of *Rhapsody in Stephen's Green* was among Flann O'Brien's papers owned by the University of Southern Illinois. But no trace until now had been found of acts two and three and a prologue and epilogue.

This play is in the vein of O'Brien's columns under the name Myles na gCopaleen (Myles of the Little Horses) for *The Irish Times* in the 1950s and 1960s, which played merry hell with his countrymen's pretensions, religious piety, political cant and official ignorance in the use of the English and Irish languages.

The first act deals with the beastly behaviour of bees and act two features avaricious beetles, greedy ducks and dopey crickets with a pronounced Cork accent. Corkmen are traditionally the butt of Dublin jokes.

But it is act three which has fascinating topical resonance. It features a colony of mindlessly driven Orange ants who work themselves into a frenzy against a colony of Green ants until finally their aggression pushes them into suicidal war with Blue ants.

The Orange ants mouth slogans such as 'The Awnt State will fieght ond the Awnt State wull be rieght!'. They also declare themselves to be 'hord-headed ond ready to fieght for the rieght to keep in stap with the Awnt Empiere'.

The phonetic spelling leaves no doubt that we are dealing with Belfast men. O'Brien, a Catholic, was actually born in Ulster, but spent most of his life in Dublin. His real name was Brian O'Nolan.

Before the Southern audience could become too smug, enter a ludicrous figure known as Deevil, transparently the prime minister Eamon de Valera, who is leader of the Green Ants and ready to march across the border to recover his property, which consists of a dead beetle.

There is no mistaking 33-year-old Brian O'Nolan's bitter disgust with the 1940s world of carnage, greed and cant at home and abroad. But on the literary level the work is rather too parochial and simplistically exhuberant to be classed as one of his major works. However it and the context in which it was born — and rapidly snuffed out — gives intriguing insights into neutral Ireland of the 1940s, suffocating in puritanism and insular politics.

The Irish Times was complimentary but *The Irish Press* was sniffy, the critic no doubt aware of the long and oppressive shadow of his proprietor, Eamon de Valera.

But the *Catholic Standard* was outraged and there were allegations that their critic, Gabriel Fallon, went to the length of trying to influence the Director of the Irish Catholic Boy Scouts to order the boys, doubling as ants and chickens, to withdraw their labour. O'Nolan was accused of presenting 'obscenities and salacities on the Dublin stage'.

We can gauge the tone of the *Catholic Standard*'s criticism by a furious letter to the paper signed 'Myles na gCopaleen': 'We protest very strongly against a dirty tirade which, under the guise of dramatic criticism, was nothing more than a treatise on dung. "There will always be a distinction," Mr Fallon says, "between the honest dung of the farmyard and nasty dirt of the chicken run."

'Personally I lack the latrine erudition to comment on this extraordinary statement, and I am not going to speculate on the odd researches that led your contributor to his great discovery. I am content to record my objection that his faecal reveries should be published.'

Whatever class of dung was involved the play did not make it into a second week and disappeared.